CRIME BEGINS AFTER SIXTY

Pistol in hand, safety catch released,
she contemplated him,
more in anger than in sorrow.
Two shots, and the man fell backward,
distinctly changed for the worse.

After that, it was no more rocking chairs.
Sid and her antique colleagues took off in a
careening black caddy with the cops in hot
pursuit—shooting at the tires. Watch them carry
out a series of audacious crimes, only one
arthritic step ahead of police, bank officials,
and the FBI—as they find the perfect solution to
old age, having a wonderful crime!

"Fast-moving . . . funny."
—*San Francisco Examiner*

About the Author

Born in Clayton, Washington, in 1909, Robert Carson is author of the best-selling *The Magic Lantern, The Revels Are Ended, Stranger in Our Midst, Quality of Mercy, Love Affair* and *My Hero*. He has also written motion pictures, including *The Light That Failed, Men with Wings* and *Bundle of Joy*. In 1937 he received an Academy Award for *A Star Is Born*. Fiction by Robert Carson has appeared in national magazines. Mr. Carson now lives with his wife Mary Jane in Los Angeles.

THE
GOLDEN YEARS
CAPER

ROBERT CARSON

 PYRAMID BOOKS • NEW YORK

TO M.J.C.

THE GOLDEN YEARS CAPER

A PYRAMID BOOK

Published by arrangement with Little, Brown and Company

Pyramid edition published October 1971

Copyright © 1970 by Robert Carson

Library of Congress Catalog Card No. 72-117038

Printed in the United States of America

Pyramid Books are published by Pyramid Communications, Inc. Its trademarks, consisting of the word "Pyramid" and the portrayal of a pyramid, are registered in the United States Patent Office. Pyramid Communications, Inc., 919 Third Avenue, New York, New York 10022

THE FIRST THING that struck you as you went by the group of ramshackle, unpainted buildings on the barren outskirts of Los Angeles was the appalling smell. It was appalling even for an area of half-depressed housing, of slaughterhouses and oil refineries. The smell was of animals and fecal matter and urine and the sweetish, terrifying corruption of death. And with the noise of trucks and industrial machinery and the hissing of valves and boilers rose a cry of sorrow, the wordless sounds of suffering beasts.

Sidney Ellen Buckner got out of her car, looked around, sniffed and listened and hesitated. She had no company at the moment. She was a neat, petite, elderly lady, small of stature, with a surprising wealth of gray hair caught up in a scarf. She was wearing nondescript slacks and a sweater and large dark glasses, and she carried a large purse.

She walked up to the place. There was no identifying sign on it. A bell jingled when she opened the gate and entered the compound. As she had anticipated, no one appeared. She went into the first building.

The stench was nearly overpowering. Starving dogs and cats, those still able to move, rose desperately from their filthy cage floors and tried to attract Sidney Ellen's attention. Others were dying or dead. The clamor grew. She blinked back tears to clear her eyes, and moved on.

Outside were more miserable creatures in chicken-wire pens, unshielded from sun or rain. The half-eaten body of a dog lay in one. A cat screamed. Beyond were buildings and pens, and a shack that constituted an office.

Mr. Jobal appeared, a fat middle-aged man, unshaven, in dirty clothing. He was a dealer in animals for experimental laboratories, and had been accused in court of giving children fifty cents or a dollar for each household pet they stole for him. His contention was that he was too poor to give proper care to his animals and that they were with him only a short time anyway. Further, he said he was innocent of making children thieves. The court had fined him fifty dollars and ordered him to change his ways. Once he was in the clear, Mr. Jobal had paid his lawyer in cash and laughed at the state humane officer who had procured the search warrant and arrested him. Then he had scowled threateningly at Sidney Ellen.

Now he stared at her, uncertain of her identity. He wasn't quite sure, and said uneasily, "Haven't I seen you before? Sure I have. What are you doing in that getup?"

"I have a reason."

"Yeah? Back again, huh? I got to admire your nerve, you old hag."

"It hasn't changed," she said.

"And it ain't going to. You think a lousy fifty-buck fine makes any difference to me?"

"I've come to plead with you, Mr. Jobal. You're a human being—I think. You could make it easier for the poor things. I'm willing to help you with the expense."

"Listen, sweetheart. You ever come on my property again and then bring a cop and pull me into court and testify against me and you're going to be real sorry."

"Mr. Jobal, how will I be sorry?"

"Never mind. You will."

The animals cried louder.

"Please, Mr. Jobal. If you'd only listen to me——"

"Beat it. Don't come back." He motioned. "If you don't want a kick in your butt, get out of here."

She contemplated him, more in anger than in sorrow.

"Listen," he said, "I'm going to make it worse for them—just because of you, you bitch. Think that over when you got a minute."

Sidney Ellen opened her purse, delved in it uncertainly and removed an automatic pistol with the barrel extended by a ventilated silencing device. There was a dry rasp resembling the warning of a serpent as her thumb released the safety catch. Jobal's eyes opened very wide and he grew rigid; a black, round hole centered on his face.

"Do you have any last words?" she asked.

"Oh, Jesus Christ, lady!" Jobal said. "No——"

"That's sufficient," she said.

The hole confronting Jobal was transferred to his head, and another was added to it. He was changed distinctly for the worse when he fell backward. Sidney Ellen engaged the safety catch, put the weapon in her purse, and strolled away. There was an amazing silence, as though the animals understood. She gazed at them for the last time, blinking again.

At the outer gate she stopped and moved behind a tall bush; a truck was passing. After that the street was deserted. She reached and entered her car, still without haste, and started it and drove off. The crying resumed, but Mr. Jobal heard nothing.

Five miles distant, having followed a circuitous route, Sidney Ellen kept a rendezvous with Major Samuel Crawford, USA (Ret.), in a sprawling, busy shopping center. By the time she came to a stop in a parking space near a J. C. Penney store, she had removed the dark glasses and scarf and gray wig, revealing neat, short-cut, permanently blond hair, and slipped out of the slacks in the midst of driving (without undue difficulty) and let down the skirts of a dress pinned up under her ample cardigan. When Sidney Ellen got out of the car to put on a coat that lay on the rear seat, her appearance was markedly changed. Leaning in and down out of general view behind the front seat, she put the pistol, wig, clothing and oddments into a large paper sack, which she carried with her, and left the car keys under the front seat.

Major Crawford was coming through the doorway of the Penney store, purchases under an arm. He was an erect, thin, bony, mean-looking man in a tweed cap, jacket and nondescript slacks. Three-quarters of an hour before he had met Sidney Ellen at a busy intersection a mile away, given her possession of the rental sedan she was driving, and had then walked to the shopping center. He did not speak, and gave her a single, questioning glance. She nodded and kept moving. Afterward she looked over her shoulder; the major was backing the car from the parking space.

At one end of the shopping center was a nursery, and there, on a pleasant pathway, selecting potted geraniums, was Mrs. Carter (Brenda) Tilden. Earlier that day Brenda had driven Major Crawford to within a block of a car rental agency in the town of Whittier, picked up Sidney Ellen at the end of a bus stop and taken her to the intersection where she was to receive the rental car from the major, and then gone to the shopping center to await the next contact. She bitterly disapproved of what Sidney Ellen, who had once played bit parts in gangster movies made in the Thirties, called "a hit." And she had not believed for a moment that there would be a hit.

"*Excuse* me," Brenda said to the Japanese salesman waiting on her. "S-sid. Wh-what have you been doing?"

"Oh, just picking up things in the market. Are you ready to go, dear?"

"Yes . . . Uh, in a minute."

Although Brenda's cheeks were whitening under her liberal makeup and her eyes were two great blue question marks under the false eyelashes, she calmly finished selecting the geraniums. Her attendant put the pots in the trunk of her Cadillac. She thanked him kindly, and he bowed and grinned.

But behind the wheel, after shifting in the seat and pulling at her girdle—Brenda was quite plump—she fumbled unsteadily with the ignition switch.

"Did you . . . What happened, Sid? Oh, dear! Don't tell me!"

"I blew his head off," Sidney Ellen said.

"Oh, Lord!"

"It's a fact."

"Sid!"

"Let's go. You have to get me to the bus line and then pick up Sam. We mustn't keep him waiting."

"I know, I know," Brenda said. "But why couldn't we have made *nice* friends when Doctor retired?"

Sidney Ellen lived in a great complex south of Long Beach which had been erected by Golden Years, Incorporated, for senior citizens. It commanded a view of the sea (from the more expensive locations) and the climate was mild. The complex was divided into four enclaves, each with a community center, and prices were scaled for the various income groups of the retired. Snug Harbor consisted of houses built around a golf course of par-three holes and was inhabited by economic royalists; their country club was full of Republicans and admirers of H. L. Hunt. Sunset Town contained smaller homes and had bowling greens but no golf course. Safe Haven had buildings that looked like dormitories with condominium apartments, and shuffleboard courts. Farthest inland, in a valley, was a community of trailers and a plain, functional center called Journey's End. Sidney Ellen, who had not prospered in her career of movie extra, stand-in, bit player and character actress, lived in Journey's End. Her aluminum trailer was smaller than many around her and she did not have attached an enclosed "ramada," an item regarded as ideal for cocktail parties and gatherings for the signing of petitions against the Golden Years management.

She had scarcely returned, changed into a muu-muu that was a relic of a trip to Hawaii two years before, when her next-door neighbor, Bill Canary, turned up. He was a thin, delicate little man with hair as blond as Sidney Ellen's (they both used the same bleach under his direction), surprisingly youthful-looking in spite of his seamed cheeks. In the remote past he had been a studio hairdresser and had known Sidney Ellen casually. At one time Bill had opened a shop in Beverly Hills known as "Coiffures by Guillaume" and gone broke.

He entered without knocking, as usual, and stood looking at Sidney Ellen with hands perched on his waist. "I've been listening to the radio," he said. "Nothing."

"He wasn't that important, Bill. Besides, they have to find him."

"You didn't really do it. Impossible!"

"It was easy," she said. "Much easier than lots of things. That's the only frightening part about it."

Bill patted his hair and sniffed. His fingers were twittery. He walked into the minuscule kitchen, sat down, and gazed up at her and sighed. She served them glasses of prepared orange juice from the refrigerator.

"It was supposed to be a joke," he said. "A dare . . . good heavens!"

"Did the auto club come about my car?"

"Yes. I was hanging around. The guy found the loose wire that led to the distributor and fixed it. He made the notations about the service call and everything."

"Good," she said. "The rest went according to plan.

Here's your gray wig. I don't think I have to get rid of the sweater and slacks, do you?"

"No . . . you remind me a little of Catherine the Great, Sid. I worked that picture—it starred Tallulah Bankhead."

"I remember. I was part of the background action in the big court scene."

"You know something?" Bill smiled slowly. "Suddenly I feel years younger!"

"So do I," she said.

Later, after a shared dinner of lamb chops and cottage cheese, Sidney Ellen and Bill took their bicycles and went to visit Dr. Tilden and Brenda at their house on the sixth green in Snug Harbor. Major Crawford was already there, Scotch and water in hand, and Biff Gagnon, a huge, bald, hearty man, once a football hero and then an insurance broker, arrived shortly and poured himself a stiff drink at the doctor's bar. Brenda appeared glum and repressed, and Sidney Ellen was elaborately demure and casual.

They discussed the weather, which was unexceptionable, and the deaths of two residents, one from Snug Harbor with emphysema and the other from Sunset Town with acute arteriosclerosis, which were also unexceptionable in their settlement. Sidney Ellen retired to the guest bathroom, fished out the pistol under her girdle, and gave it to the major.

All eyes were on the gun. Sam opened the breech, extracted a cartridge, and removed the magazine and counted the remaining rounds.

"Five bullets," he commented. "Were you wild, Sid?"

"Not a bit," she said. "Your instructions were perfect. I took an easy stance and extended my arm and pretended I was pointing the gun as I would my finger. Each shot was squeezed off. I think I got him twice as he was going down."

"Son of a gun!" Biff Gagnon said.

"Nothing beats a twenty-two magnum," Sam said. "You can't do better than a small piece with limited recoil and the most highly developed cartridge known. Even the damned Army finally found that out in Vietnam. All you have to do is aim for a vital spot, particularly the head—that always finishes 'em whether you make a bull's-eye or not."

"That's where I aimed," Sidney Ellen said.

"The hollow-nose bullets—were they effective?"

"Well, I didn't look closely, but he sure was a mess." Sam showed satisfaction. "I'm proud of you, Sid."

"I never thought you'd go through with it," Biff said. He seemed queasy.

"I always meant to from the moment you said why not kill him, and that I didn't really have the guts."

"Well, this is a great day," Biff said. "I think I'll have another belt of Carter's medicine. . . ."

"Please do," the doctor said. "You have a little trauma, I think."

They felt a sudden, gushing, pleasurable excitement. It was new and strange. Living in Golden Years and aging was awfully dull. Only Brenda was not amused.

"Do *any* of you realize you're talking about a *murder?*" she demanded, and got up. "I'm going to bed, if you'll *please* pardon me!"

"Don't mind us, dear," Bill said acidly. "You're merely the hostess."

Dr. Tilden watched Brenda leave. He was by far the oldest of the group—he would not disclose his age, but he was reputed to be seventy-eight or nine—and he had a long, expressionless face and a domed, hairless head and pale eyes magnified behind thick spectacle lenses. His first wife had died years before and Brenda was a fairly youthful successor, an appointments nurse from the last office he had maintained, in Portland, Oregon, before his retirement.

"She always contributes a jarring note to anything,"

he remarked. "At first she wasn't going to work for me because I was a proctologist. . . . I'm sorry."

"Let's say she's rather conventional," Sam said.

"Her interests are limited," Carter Tilden said. "She's had only the equivalent of a high school education, and her responses are typical—she can't envisage anything beyond clothing, furs, automobiles and trying unsuccessfully to keep her weight down."

"Well, she's young and flighty," Biff said, and grinned. "She's only pushing fifty, isn't she, Doc?"

"Forty-six, I think," Carter said. "Lately I've heard her telling people she's going to be forty her next birthday. I don't contradict her."

Sam wrapped the pistol in a cloth and put it in a dispatch case beside his chair. "I expect I'd better disassemble this piece completely," he said. "You can go to jail for having a firearm fitted with a silencer."

"Also for murdering somebody with it," Biff added.

"I can't believe anyone saw me," Sid said. "To tell you the truth, I don't actually care. Jobal was a terrible man—he won't be missed. And now those poor animals will be taken by the SPCA and given decent care or put to sleep. You'd come to prison to see me, wouldn't you?"

"We'd all be there with you, luv," Bill said. "We're accessories after the fact."

"I'll tell you something else," Sid went on. "It's not only that I'm not afraid or that my conscience doesn't bother me or that I didn't hesitate a second in shooting him . . . the honest truth is *I liked doing it.*" She paused. "I got us started. Now what?"

"I don't know," Carter said. "Let's think a moment. It seems to me that we supported Sid quite well. Presumably no one saw her or took her license number. Even if somebody did, he observed a different person and the car was rented by the major in another town. He used an assumed name and showed false credentials and will be virtually impossible to find. Each of us has an alibi. Sam says twenty-two-caliber bullets are the hardest to identify in ballistics tests—if the gun is ever discovered. But the police may call on Sid. Remember she has been connected with the victim while hauling him into court."

"You'll have to be cool, luv," Bill said.

"I'm not much of an actress," she said, "but I'm good enough to play that part."

"I must say I don't see any loose ends," Sam said. "Our transfers took place in crowded localities. The auto club will verify that Sid's car was out of action. She did take the bus to Long Beach to go shopping, where she met Brenda by accident—and Brenda was just out as always tooling her car around and shopping. I hitched a ride to the stores with her and bought a few things and came home on the bus. The rest of the day I spent with Dr. Tilden."

"I remember that vividly," Carter said.

"I spent the day on the golf course," Bill said. "For real."

"Me," Bill said, "I was in my little tin house sewing and putting up new curtains. For real."

Carter got small brandies for himself and Sid, and lit his pipe. Biff had another bourbon on the rocks.

"It doesn't appear too difficult, eh?" Carter asked. "Provided this has been a fair example of how to put together an unlawful enterprise, and I think it is."

"You need, I suppose," Sam said, "what they call in the spy novels a good cover. What could be better than being elderly and living in Golden Years?"

"And no police record," Biff said. "We're all clean. . . . Could you ask for more?"

"A bit more," Carter said. "Strength, youth and good eyesight, for instance—and considerably more spryness."

"I can still do a hundred-pound press," Biff said.

"Look at it this way," Sam said. "A small-caliber

piece with a rapid rate of fire is a great equalizer. And brains and experience ought to make up for some of our physical defects."

"That's true," Carter agreed. "Long ago I had a residency in a county hospital, and among other duties I serviced the prison ward and had patients in the county jail. The low level of intelligence and education among crooks was very apparent to me. Except for a few old cons who were born losers and the usual victims of passion or accident, they were young and dumb and at the mercy of their ignorance, misguided instincts and vainglory. The successful murderers and thieves were all on the outside, in business and government and the armed forces and brokerage houses. No wonder the ordinary lawbreaker gets caught."

"It takes a certain resolution, I guess," Sam said. "A real purpose, too. I know we're all sore at the world, but what are we after?"

"Loot," Bill replied. "You have an Army pension, Major, and the doctor is well off, but what about the rest of us? Do you think we're dancing in the streets with our hundred and ninety dollars a month or less and the chance to pay five bucks a month to Medicare and make out those wonderful forms? Do you think we *like* to be kept from working so we can keep on drawing that kind of money? Especially when every day we can read in the paper how some long-haired kid singing folk-rock through his adenoids has just signed a contract for a million and Howard Hughes owns Nevada and Onassis has gone off in his yacht again with the little woman wearing rubies and that they slapped Dean Witter on the wrist for peddling some advance information on McDonnell-Douglas?"

Carter puffed his pipe. When Sid admiringly remarked that he looked a little like Allen Dulles, Carter said Dulles was dead and he probably should be.

"Everybody is waiting for that," Bill said. "It isn't

always a long wait. Shouldn't we stir up a little excitement while we're hanging around?"

"That's right," Sid said. "It isn't as if we were among *friends*."

"Very well," Carter decided. "Let's try to find a new project."

Brenda suddenly appeared, in robe and nightgown, her hair intricately laced through a number of large plastic cylinders and wetted with a substance that smelled sour.

"I can't sleep with the conversation going on," she said. "Carty, when are you coming to bed?"

"Soon," he told her.

"And what is Murder, Incorporated doing?" she asked. "Getting ready to kill somebody else?"

"No, this will be for money," Sid said. "Probably no one will get hurt."

"What?" Brenda cried.

"Go back to bed," Carter said.

"I want an explanation of what Sid just said to me!"

"The explanation is this: we're interested in founding a profit-making organization. Goodnight."

"I'll do your hair for you tomorrow, dear," Bill said. "You're going to have a rat's nest when you get up. But don't bother us now."

Staring at them, clutching at her encumbered head, Brenda said, "You're not kidding. Oh, my God. And to think Carty and I had to come here for peace and quiet and then meet you in the shuffleboard tournaments!"

It was true. Biff had won the singles title for Safe Haven, the Tildens briefly represented Snug Harbor, and Sid and Bill lasted until the third round playing for Journey's End.

Next morning there was a brief mention in the Los Angeles newspaper of the discovery of the body of Herman Jobal, proprietor of a kennel in the southeastern part of the city. Several bullets had pierced him in what appeared to be a typical gangland-style execution. Police had ruled out robbery as a motive, since the deceased had retained possession of his wallet and other valuables. Recently Mr. Jobal had been a defendant in a court action with respect to the condition of the animals in his care.

Jobal's passing was also noted on television and radio news programs, but in an even briefer style. Thereafter he was never heard of again.

Sid nerved herself for a possible encounter with the cops. Programs she had seen on TV, as well as movies, led her to expect that quiet, intent young men in plain clothes would visit her and ask polite, barbed questions. Or the detectives might bring her to a grim stationhouse and grill her relentlessly. She resolved to be her most feminine and vague.

But there was not as much as a telephone call. Mr. Jobal, gratifyingly full of holes in the head, vanished unhonored and unsung. The obvious explanation was both comforting and a little irksome: the authorities simply didn't believe little old ladies devoted to the welfare of animals were capable of direct action. Or, no doubt, their aging male counterparts. Crime, like everything else in America, belonged to youth.

BIFF PROVIDED the first interesting lead, but it had to be acted upon immediately. Although opposed to haste, Carter—who was instinctively looked to as spokesman for the group, perhaps because he was senior to the others and the most learned and successful of them—felt disposed to consider the project on the ground that it was in Biff's province of insurance, where he had prospered for years trading on his athletic reputation.

During a weekend golfing trip to Palm Springs, Biff had chanced to hear a Sunday afternoon radio program conducted by a sprightly lady on a local station, whose specialty was taped interviews with unusual or prominent visitors to the desert area. The broadcast was about a visit she had made on West Stevens Road in the Las Palmas district to a house temporarily occupied by Mr. Henry Hoven, a representative of Wycroft & Benz, the international jewelry firm with salesrooms in New York, London, Paris and Rome. Hoven's function was the personal servicing of important and favored clients. He dealt only in exceptional, very expensive items. Each year he made the rounds of exclusive watering places and attended the beautiful people on his list. Naturally he carried with him many fine pieces, as well as photographs and descriptions of Wycroft & Benz's complete stock.

Hoven welcomed the exposure and talked freely to his interviewer. He had another week to go in his rented quarters and solicited inquiries from qualified purchasers; he revealed his telephone number and address and described the valuables he had on hand, including diamonds, rubies and emeralds in clips, brooches, bracelets and rings, as well as numerous unset stones for which the superb craftsmen of Wycroft & Benz would be happy to design original settings. All showings were by appointment, in dignity and seclusion. No appointments were possible after five P.M.; Hoven devoted evenings to his social rounds, which he intimated were considerable.

"This is a special service," he explained, "limited to the best people—people who can afford the finest."

In response to a question, Hoven said he had never been robbed and never expected to be. He took sensible precautions. His stock was not transported by him, but sent from town to town by registered mail. Each night his cases of jewels were put in the safe or vault of some business friend for storage. During the day he was protected by an off-duty policeman hired at every stop.

Laughing, he added: "My firm has plenty of insurance. Anyway, the jewelry is so distinctive, the uncut stones so well known in the trade, that no thief would be able to dispose of them. Wycroft & Benz designs are immediately recognizable to anyone who knows fine things."

"That's what interested me," Biff said during the meeting Carter called at his house. "The insurance part. They're plastered with it. I know the company—National Guardian."

"I don't follow you," Carter said.

"Here's what I mean," Biff said. "I realize you're going to say we can't handle jewelry—that we're not equipped to get rid of it and so forth. My point is we don't. We don't have to."

"Why not?"

"Because insurance companies are just as crooked and unwilling to pay as everybody thinks they are. When they have a big loss their main concern is to settle for as little as possible. Now, Henry Hoven is probably toting upwards of a quarter of a million around with him. National Guardian is liable for a total loss that could make them put up a wailing wall in their New York office. Ordinary thieves don't worry them too much—they could count on getting most of the stuff back through fences, pawnshops and underworld informants. But what if they ran up against a different kind of operator, a guy who has no intention of disposing of the rocks except by flushing them down the toilet if they refuse to pay? Guess what Guardian would do after they got the bad news."

"Would they believe that?"

"Why not? And they couldn't afford to take a chance if you offered them a good price."

"It sounds like a new idea," Sam commented. "The main advantage, and safety, is not having to sell the stuff. And I'm mean enough to enjoy destroying it if we get turned down by Guardian."

"Anything done to an insurance company is in the public interest," Bill said.

"I think you're all nuts!" Brenda said.

"But have we time to pull it off?" Carter said. "Only a week . . ."

"Maybe you have," Biff said with pride, "on account of little me. I've cased the job. The house is up for rent again, and I got a realtor to take me by Sunday night while Hoven was out. Then I phoned Hoven Monday morning, gave a fake name, and made a date for friends of mine coming in from Chicago to see him at four-thirty next Friday afternoon."

"Not so good," Bill said. "Now they could recognize you. Does the realtor have your real name?"

"No. He meets a hundred people a week—how

would he remember me, a guy in dark glasses and a planter's hat? It just means I won't ever go to Palm Springs again and can't be in on the robbery."

Bill sniffed. "That's a handy out."

"Don't get nasty, bright eyes. Somebody has to furnish the brains and skill."

There was a lengthy discussion. Brenda took no part in it, and several times held up a hand and disdainfully inspected her fingernails. Biff described in detail the house on Stevens Road. Stoking his pipe, Carter thought he might go down to the Springs the following day for a preliminary survey; his words caused Brenda to brighten.

"Can I drive you?" she asked.

"Yes," he said ungraciously. "That's all you're good for, dear."

"If we do it," Sam said, "what would we ask?"

"A hundred thousand," Biff said. "Settle for fifty. Don't be too greedy and scare them off."

Brenda's interest was aroused. "I wish we could keep the jewels," she said, "even if I am out of my head in talking to you ding-a-lings. I've always wanted some nice emeralds."

"You'll never have any," Carter said. "Forget it. This is purely a business venture."

"Oh, pooh!" Brenda said.

Dr. Tilden went to Palm Springs to inspect the location of the house on Stevens Road. It occupied a corner; there were several vacant lots across the street, and the nearest house on that side was secluded and a considerable distance away. The house next door to the north was not tenanted, though of course it might be the coming weekend. The house on the opposing corner also seemed empty. Hoven's house was conveniently screened by a low wall and high oleander bushes planted inside it. The doctor carefully traced and followed an escape route for leaving town that first went north and then joined the freeway out of Palm Springs.

Brenda wanted to stay overnight, but she could not sway her husband. "You know what?" she said. "You've become an old fool."

"Senile dementia," he said.

"You are going to jail, mark my words."

"And you with me."

"Oh, no! Not me. I haven't done anything."

"Not yet."

"This is the craziest thing you've ever done!"

"It's nothing compared to my marrying a second time."

She glared at him. "You want my honest opinion, Carty? The part of human beings you had to look at all your life did something to you. You're not quite with it. . . . That's the unkindest cut of all, isn't it?"

"Exactly what my patients always said," he retorted. "Shut up."

When he returned to Snug Harbor, Carter called another meeting. He was for the venture. The principal snag lay in the collection of tribute—the manner and means. That was settled satisfactorily. A mantlepiece clock ticked on as, long past their customary early bedtimes, they went over and over details. Personnel were chosen: Sam and Sid, Carter, and Brenda for the driving.

Brenda, yawning and aghast, stiffened. "Me?" she cried. "Are you kidding? In our sixty-nine Caddy? I wouldn't even consider it!"

"Go to your room, please, my dear," Carter said.

Bursting into tears, blinded by running mascara, she left them. They wearily watched her go.

"She is observing the longest menopause I ever heard of," Bill said.

"Well, she's a good driver," Sam said.

"I wonder . . ." Sid ventured. "She just doesn't seem to fit in, does she? Maybe we ought to——"

"No," Carter interrupted sharply. "It isn't feasible for her to withdraw now, and we need her."

Sam smiled. "We could have Sid pay a call on her, the kind Mr. Jobal had."

Everybody gave a start, and no smile answered Sam's.

"That's not in awfully good taste, Major," Sid said.

"Perhaps not," Sam replied. "But this isn't a sewing circle. Have the rest of you ever really considered that?"

They were silent.

"It is not a bad idea," Carter said thoughtfully. "However, for the moment I must decline even well-meant offers to make me a widower."

As she pedaled back to Journey's End with Bill that night, through deserted streets and past the unlighted houses, apartments and trailers full of their sleeping, worn occupants, Sidney Ellen began to smile. Sam's words abided with her. It damn well wasn't a sewing circle! These other people would arise tomorrow and the day after that and the day after that, and for God knew how long until the Dark Angel overtook them. Condemned to gossip, inactivity, boredom, silly games and the dubious joys of watching photographic slides on travel at the camera club and listening to lectures in the main assembly hall by flower arrangers and aggressive men running for minor municipal offices on reform tickets. But she had been freed. She was a killer, and she was going to Palm Springs, gun in hand, to try to win a fortune, just as if she were twenty again and like the Bonnie of that wonderful movie. Fear salted her anticipation, and she perceived that it was essential to life, as were chance and the imminence of violence and the lures of sin, and gave living a proper taste.

"What are you grinning for?" Bill asked.

"Oh, I'm enjoying myself. Time passes so slowly when you settle down! Now it's going fast again."

"Yeah, things have speeded up, haven't they?"

"You know," she said. "I was pretty once."

"You're pretty now, luv."

"Not anymore, Bill. Im wrinkled and I sag here and there, and when I don't wear my contact lenses I can't see very well. But I wasn't always this way. I had a good figure from dancing in musicals and my face wasn't bad."

"I remember."

"I might have been a star. Girls made it with less than I had. They slept with the right men and got a break. I was too picky or fastidious or whatever it was. Good Lord, I was proud of that—and ended up calling Central Casting every morning!"

"Being decent is not how to get ahead in anything," Bill said. "The trouble is, you don't catch on to that until it's too late." He grunted, pushing down on the pedals. "No wonder the kids are sore these days and hollering about telling it like it is. Think of all the goody-goody crap they laid on us."

"Ummm . . . Maybe I could have had lovers and clothes and money and publicity. At least I could have claimed I got somewhere. Do you think it would have been better?"

"Sure."

"The funny thing is," she said, "when I'd saved myself and kept my nose clean and had a husband and stayed in the kitchen, he got tired of me and wanted a divorce. Bill, is there a moral?"

"Absolutely. The moral is, don't be moral."

She sighed. "Well, it was a long time ago."

They stopped at her trailer. Bill started to say goodnight.

"Come in for a moment," she said. "I'm too excited to sleep."

"I'm not," Bill said. "It's far beyond my bedtime already. If I don't keep regular hours my complexion goes and no amount of beauty treatments will bring it back. So long, luv."

[24]

THURSDAY MORNING Sidney Ellen encountered Biff at the Golden Years Supermarket, which was near the entrance to the complex. They met at the meat cold box, where Biff was carefully inspecting steaks through their transparent wrappings.

"Hi," he said. "Got to keep that old protein flowing through me, building up the muscle. I put out a lot of energy."

"To tell you the truth," she said, "I can't afford them too often unless I want to give up movies and perfume. My speed is creamed tuna on toast and vegetable salads."

"I can't afford them either, but how would I have the energy to take money away from these suckers? Lately I've been playing pool over at Sunset Town community center. The major introduced me. I'm on my feet all day."

"You may not have to do that much longer."

They exchanged glances and lowered their voices.

"Maybe not," Biff said. "Maybe I can buy a whole steer, prime grade, and put it in a freeze locker. Tomorrow's the big day, huh?"

"Yes. Don't you wish you were going?"

"Yeah." He frowned. "Why should I snow you, Sid? No, I don't. I'm glad to be out of it."

"Come on."

"True, kid. I'm a mass of muscle and cowardice. The waiting kills me. Before a game I used to have loose bowels. That's why I never cared to play pro ball."

"Then why did you get into this?"

"I don't know. Oh, I was a hero for a little while. They patted me on the back and couldn't do enough for me. But the bastards dropped me just when I was getting to like it. That was like falling off a cliff. I spent the rest of my life sucking around them with my hat in my hand."

"I'm sorry, Biff. Everbody gets his lumps."

"Yeah," he said, and his heavy face flushed. "But I'd like to get even. Listen, do you think this top sirloin would be tough?"

"Use tenderizer," she said. "See you later."

While she pushed a metal cart and collected a few staples from the shelves, she pondered on the incredible circumstances of the six of them getting together and the even more unbelievable sequence of compatibilities, ideas, prejudices, disillusionments, hidden rages and daydreams.

Shuffleboard was the instigator of their acquaintanceship. But half the old crocks in Golden Years—over a thousand of them—were in the tournaments, often to part in ill will and scarcely exchange greetings again.

Out of the many people, how had six (five, really, for poor Brenda had to be discounted) of the most disaffected . . . happened to meet and form a common purpose?

Each of them mourned a wasted youth and dull middle years, and dreaded a sorry, ignominious end. No doubt they had more energy and malice than their peers—and more courage. They hated their environment and all its newest manifestations. Their instinct was to strike back against every past deluding, fleecing, abasement, boredom, neglect, regimentation, disappointment, frustration and slight, including a final casual removal to a boneyard. Like the youthful they hated and feared and envied, probably they also were spoiled by a mechanistic and impersonal civilization. The dead weight of bureaucracy and a stifling welfare state crushed them too. If the world was coming to an end—and who could say it wasn't?—then the finish was of no consequence to them and hastening it would provide great satisfaction.

But where was the moment of decision? That evaded Sid, and she had a good memory and a mind for detail. Of course her blind rage with Jobal and intemperate words and the challenge (a word applied to everything these days) offhandedly presented to her caused this. Much had gone before, though, and a hidden, comforting community of interest and gathering intention found among them. There were long talks of their helplessness and sense of imprisonment, of bloodthirsty dreams and little cruelties committed that could have been big ones, of a lust for vengeance that was part of being human. And violence and revolt was in the air. They lived in a century of war, wholesale slaughter, apocalyptic bombs, torture, well-publicized injustice and hatred, and the destruction of the moral values which had precariously held creation together for a few thousand years.

Anarchy was the order of the day. On television, boys were killed and maimed in Asia and hapless villagers massacred and seared with jellied petroleum, and fictional characters settled their disputes with gun and knife and inflicted brutal beatings. In the emancipated movies handsome, glamorous people committed crimes, fornicated, paraded their nudity and slew enemies without compassion. The police beat raging mobs with clubs and choked them with tear gas. Students closed and ravaged universities. Air was foul and thick, the earth was defiled, streams and rivers and oceans were polluted. A torrent of babies promised starvation before long; another torrent of automobiles promised to stop all movement and asphyxiate everybody. Women wore clothing that scarcely covered their hips. The rich were richer, the poor poorer. And the blacks vowed to get whitey. The streets weren't safe at night. Jeremiahs and scientists and disgruntled politicians out of power predicted a quick finish. Meanwhile, citizens burned the flag and went on strike and debased the currency and used obfuscating words like "infrastructure," "confrontation," "underachievement" and "escalation." Everything was buggered up beyond all recognition.

It just made you mad, Sidney Ellen thought. If you had any guts, you tried to get even.

At the checkstand she smiled and had her purchases totaled and paid the amount on the cash register tape and got her Blue Chip stamps, a pleasant, diminutive, harmless old party from the unchic section of Journey's End.

Bill Canary presided over the final preparations that Thursday night at Major Crawford's house in Sunset Town, which the major had kept after the sudden death of his wife because of the odds and ends he had accumulated during his long tour of duty in the Army at home and abroad and because of the little machine shop rigged in his garage. On his fireplace were crossed Moro bolos; he owned a collection of Chinese jade, firearms both antique and modern from several countries, a shrunken head out of the Amazon country, scrimshaw, a South Sea idol of imposing ugliness, and much china gathered by the late Mrs. Crawford.

"It's all I've got," he said, "to show for a lifetime of discipline and devotion to duty—unless you want to count the permanent rank of major, a government pittance, free burial at Arlington if the Kennedys don't take up all the space, and free medical attention from service doctors I wouldn't trust to treat me for a thick callus. I got kicked out, you know—too long in grade, passed over, had to make room for the young ones.

Never mind that I was in three wars and knew more about ordnance than anybody. I was a mustang—up through the ranks—and so I didn't come from a class at West Point that produced a lot of generals or have a ring or know anybody or wear my garrison cap down on my nose. The establishment goes on inside as well as out, friends. Noses are even browner, if you know what I mean. In the Air Force everybody is a bird colonel, but I was lucky to even get into field grade. My failing was that I gave straight answers, didn't kiss the right backsides, and kept my self-respect. Oh, hell. Never mind. But they're not going to make me fade away!"

Bill had been a makeup man on the old poverty row productions before he became a hair stylist, and he had brought a couple of cartons of specialties for changing the appearance of the task force. Sam had set up two bridge tables, mostly to deceive and outsiders who might drop in, but they were not used. Sullen at first, Brenda grew childishly absorbed when she learned she was to have a black wig, dark glasses and a heavy application for her face, neck, arms and hands that would give her the look of being deeply tanned. She stood raptly in front of a mirror in the spare bedroom contemplating the change Bill had wrought.

"It certainly is *interesting*," she said. "But I simply don't look my best with dark hair, do I, Carty?"

"Oh, shut up," Carter said. He had a rubberized extension to his nose, a curly brown toupee, and Bill had asked him to remove his upper plate to change the contours of his face; all this made him irritable and uncomfortable, and thickened his speech.

"Bill," Brenda said, ignoring her husband. "You've got to fix it. I'm *too* black. They might take me for a colored person."

"So much the better," Bill replied. "Wear an old, loose dress, dear, and a ratty coat. They'll think you're somebody's maid."

"Well, I like *that!*" Brenda said. "What do you think I am?"

"Well, to start with, sweetheart," Bill began, "I think—"

"Knock it off," Sam said. "We haven't got time for personal evaluations." A thin plastic addition to his head had covered his pepper-and-salt hair, giving him a monk's tonsure and fluffy white fuzz to encircle it; a white moustache was pasted to his upper lip, and Bill had painted dark circles under his eyes.

Sid wore the gray wig again, and, her contact lenses discarded, thick-rimmed spectacles; her normal cosmetics were scrubbed off, her plucked eyebrows thickened, and she was instructed to adopt a shuffling walk, bow her shoulders, and clothe herself in loose garments and, inevitably, tennis shoes.

"It beats me," Biff said, in wonderment. "I wouldn't know any of you. The three of you look ancient, and Brenda looks like a spade."

"Carty!" Brenda said. "I won't do it! Not in black-face!"

"I'm dazzlingly clever," Bill said, "but I can't restore your youth. Only Elizabeth Arden can do that. You'd all better rehearse the makeup again. When you put on the disguises tomorrow in a hurry you've got to be letter-perfect."

Despite protests, Brenda was compelled to go through the motions with the rest of them. Then she cried and made rivulets on her darkened face. Nobody bothered to console her.

"Okay," Bill said. "I've done my part. I'll assemble the kits for you; the wardrobe is your problem."

Biff kept consulting his watch. In an afterthought, Carter had insisted on establishing a complete alibi: they were to meet Biff (he would be prepared to swear) in San Diego for a day of sightseeing, and they had to pick him up there at a rendezvous when the job was finished. The taxi was coming for him any minute;

he had to catch a plane at Long Beach Airport. Presently they heard the sound of a car outside.

"Lots of luck, kids," Biff said. "I'll be waiting for you and praying."

"Just wait for us," Carter snapped.

After Biff left, Sam distributed weapons and checked a miniature toolcase he was to carry. Sid was given the gun she had used on Jobal, Carter an imposing 7 mm. Luger intended for display purposes, and Sam reserved for himself a reworked .22 caliber automatic pistol with an enlarged magazine, special forward grip and the capability of fully automatic firing. Carter put the Luger in his hip pocket. Flinching at the contact of cold metal on her skin, Sid slipped the pistol into her girdle; discomfort notwithstanding, it felt reassuring. She thought they were on firm psychological ground in all those westerns and gangster movies—packing a gun did something for your confidence.

"Meeting adjourned," Carter said. "Goodnight, everybody."

"Good hunting," Bill said. "That's what they always said to the pilots in those Royal Air Force war pictures."

Sam smiled faintly. "I had a CO back in the dark ages—so help me, he'd fought Indians once. He called the enemy 'hostiles.' We're surrounded by 'em."

"All right," Bill said. "Take care of the hostiles, Major."

"Which reminds me," Sam said. "When we pull these pieces we may have to use them. If I open up, I expect to be supported. Understand?"

Carter and Sid nodded. At the door, tears again overwhelmed Brenda. Carter spoke loudly: "My wife takes contract too seriously, Sam. A lovely evening. Thank you."

He gripped his wife's arm and escorted her to their car. Picking up the bicycles, Sid and Bill made their goodbyes. No neighbors seemed to be observing them.

"That fat frump worries me," Bill said, when they were under way. "She's all wrong for the part."

"We might have to open up on *her.*" Sid said grimly.

They were a grumpy lot in the morning, edgy, sourstomached, conscious of having slept fitfully. The ebullience of the preceding evening had vanished. Behind her dark glasses Brenda was evidently tearful, for she kept sniffing and dabbing at her nose with a handkerchief; but she drove with her customary skill as they headed toward San Diego for a few minutes to fortify their alibi. Then, on Carter's instructions, she swung around and went toward the desert, via Pasadena and San Bernardino. In the upland country he selected a deserted road for her to turn onto, and an area screened by trees and scrub where they could put on their disguises.

This required time; they were slow and clumsy, especially the men. Only Sidney Ellen was fairly adept, and she had to aid the others. A small boy and his dog passed by, forcing them to halt operations, and it seemed that he eyed them suspiciously as he paused, almost disposed to a conversation. Sam glared at him and shook his head, and the boy moved on.

"I hope he's not old enough to remember license plates," he muttered.

"Or people who look as though they were getting ready for a Hallowe'en party," Sid said, and they all felt a premonitory chill.

As soon as the boy was out of sight, they finished the changes, and Sam removed the license plates, secured by handy wing nuts, and Carter gummed a temporary paper license on the rear window of the car and a small folded temporary registration slip to the inside of the lower right quadrant of the windshield. His habit of buying a new Cadillac every year, and Brenda's devoted automotive care, made the illusion believable.

An argument erupted when Sid suggested Brenda add more dark makeup. She refused flatly.

"I am not going to Palm Springs and be a colored person," she said. "Why, they hardly let them in town."

When they returned to the road two sportive, hairy youths on light motorcycles passed them, cackling and making curious gestures—they slowed down and looked back, and appeared a trifle threatening to the ancients. Sam picked up the gun he kept in a shopping bag.

"Overpopulation," he said. "We could help correct that . . . ."

Afterward Sid speculated on how surprised the two bearded hoodlums would have been—for the last time, of course—if they had elected to try to stop the shiny sedan. She was not much disturbed at the prospect of riddling them with soft-cone bullets. You had to think in practical terms: they might recall salient details, including a license number, with far less difficulty than the boy.

A late lunch provided the test for their disguises. The step was taken deliberately, for although they looked passable to one another, there was the possibility that they were being deludedly optimistic. Their stop was at a drive-in stand in Indio, where they had gone without pausing in Palm Springs to use up time. Watching narrowly, they observed that the girl who brought their trays of hamburgers and coffee didn't give them a second glance, nor did the tourists and necking high school kids parked around them. Emboldened, Carter surreptitiously put in his upper denture to facilitate eating and later removed it. The gasoline station attendant on the highway who refueled the car did not display curiosity either; Brenda, having been warned by her husband, paid cash instead of using a credit card.

Shadows lengthened on the desert. The sun began to sink behind the towering granite pinnacles of the San Jacinto Mountains. Traffic was heavy on the main streets of Palm Springs, and the sidewalks were thronged with elderly winter visitors, men in flowered loose shirts and shorts and socks and shoes, accompanied by their wives in sunsuits and muu-muus. Carter would not permit Brenda to stop.

"It looks so nice," she said wistfully. "I wish we could come here sometime and stay for a month. I'd like to get a good tan."

"You've got a better tan than any of them," he replied.

"Oh, Carty!"

He consulted his watch and directed her to Stevens Road.

They pulled on their gloves and perspired. Sid ground her teeth and Sam clenched and unclenched his fists. Carter puffed out his sunken cheeks. The air Brenda gulped caused her to belch.

"Pardon *me*," she said in a small voice.

She brought the car to a stop in front of the house Carter indicated. Two cars of lower-priced makes stood in the carport—no doubt a rental sedan for Mr. Hoven, and the one belonging to his police attendant. The early violet dusk had fallen and the air was chilling. There were no streetlights, and no signs of people moving about. A foreign sports car went noisily by at considerable speed, driven by a girl with glamorous long blond tresses flying in the wind. From the house up the way on the opposite side came the sound of music and voices—a radio playing. The side intersection did not extend farther than Stevens Road, and the house on that corner looked dark and empty. To the extent they could see through shrubbery, the house next door was also untenanted.

"Leave the engine running, Brenda," Carter said. "All right. Let's go."

"My God." Brenda said. "I think I'm going to be sick."

The three of them walked up to the door somewhat

too hastily, jostling each other, and Sam pressed the button. Chimes rang. In the doorway appeared a small, neat, sunburned man, thin-haired, clad in a tieless Brooks Brothers plaid shirt and fawn-colored trousers; on his feet were leather sandals of the same shade as his pants.

"Good evening," the man said. "I'm Henry Hoven." The overhead entrance light had gone on as he came to answer their summons, and he seemed surprised by the trio confronting him. "Are you the Burtons from Chicago?"

"Yes," Sam said. He gestured toward Carter. "This is Mr. Smithson, a friend. Are we too early?"

"Not at all, sir," Hoven assured him. "You are my last appointment for the day. Please come in."

He stood aside, smiling at Sidney Ellen, and she beamed at him charmingly, gripping the butt of the pistol inside her coat with damp palm and fingers. Sam and Carter followed; Hoven closed the door.

"I hope you won't mind the informality of my attire, Mrs. Burton," he said. "One dresses for the desert, eh?" He twinkled. "But I wouldn't want this to get back to the august precincts of Wycroft & Benz."

"Well, as you can see," Sid responded, in steady tones that astonished her, "we appreciate roughing it here, too. In Chicago it seems we are always in formal attire for one thing or another."

"Yes, many of my clients complain of the social grind," Hoven said. "Won't you sit down, please? I'll be happy to bring my little collection for your pleasure."

They seated themselves as planned, at strategic intervals commanding all angles. Biff's description and rough sketch of the premises had been accurate and complete. The double-size living room had a hanging fireplace in its center and planters on either side; beyond was a lanai with bamboo furniture and a bar, and solid glass walls that gave out on lawn and grass and a swimming pool and dressing rooms in a small structure. Garden lights glowed softly. A doorway to the left permitted a view into a bedroom, and next to it was a hallway leading to the kitchen and service area, and servant's quarters; on the right side of the living room was another hallway admitting on more bedrooms—from that section a television set could be heard playing softly. The central heating was on, and the thermostatically controlled blower, coming into operation at intervals, made a distinct booming noise.

In the right hall doorway came a bulky young man in his shirtsleeves and civilian attire, except for a small holster holding a snub-nosed revolver clipped to his belt; he glanced at them briefly, and disappeared.

"It's that relaxing hour," Hoven said. "May I offer you a little liquid hospitality?"

"Mr. Burton and I are on a health plan," Sid said, "and not drinking. The round of parties before we left Chicago almost killed us." She smiled again. "We're not as young as we once were, you know."

"One would never know it, Mrs. Burton," Hoven said. "Mr. Smithson?"

"No, thanks," Carter replied thickly. "I've got dental troubles, Mr. Hoven."

"I'm sorry to hear that, sir," Hoven said. "Then perhaps we ought to get right down to the purpose of your visit. May I have an idea of what you are looking for?"

"Something elegant," Sid said. "Our forty-fifth anniversary is coming up and Mr. Burton has promised me the best." She giggled. "And Mr. Smithson can afford not to stint on his married daughters."

"Ah . . ." Hoven said, and got up. "Congratulations. Excuse me."

He went to the bar, on which were placed several cases bound in red morocco, selected two of them, and returned to spread and open them on a coffee table before Sid. She and Carter fixed eyes on Sam, who arose and moved forward, keeping the right hall under surveillance.

The cases had trays in them; Hoven spread these out for inspection. "Here's a diamond necklace I might recommend for madame," he said. "Platinum and eighteen-cart gold, with cabochon emeralds and rubies. Or these diamond geese in flight . . . The emerald-cut diamond set in a platinum ring may interest you. And I have this absolutely unique sapphire-, aquamarine- and diamond-studded necklace. Matching earrings go with it. . . . Or would you prefer marquise-cut diamonds, up to nearly any size as you can see here, put in your own custom-designed setting?"

His treasures sparkled and glittered in the lamplight, emitting golden, green, blue, crimson, purple and translucently white rays; then came the dull shine of gun metal. Sam's weapon centered on Hoven. The heating plant had come on. Carter and Sid promptly drew their pistols. Hoven had (Carter thought) the expression of a man who had just incurred an inguinal hernia—mingled pain, fear and pitiful surprise compounded in approximately equal parts.

"Call your cop," Sam whispered, "and make it casual —as if you're finishing with us."

Hoven started to speak, eyed the guns, and thought better of it. He called, with commendable calm, "Oh, Jerry—we're finished. Will you come in?"

Summoned by a jerk of Sam's head, Carter arose and joined him at the entrance to the right hallway. Sid covered Hoven, who stared at her reproachfully.

The sound of the TV stopped, and the large young man materialized and froze, very astonished.

"You wouldn't want to get killed, would you, son?" Sam asked.

"No," the cop said. "That a machine pistol you got?"

"Yes," Sam said. "So you just unclip that fancy fast-draw holster without trying to show us how good it works and toss it on the sofa there. Don't move a bit fast."

Unhurriedly, the cop complied with the order. Carter

picked up the holstered revolver and put it in his pocket. He crossed to the bar, drew two glasses of water, and returned to where Sid, who had risen, and Sam were silently herding Hoven and the cop to seated positions together on another sofa. Carter put the glasses in front of them on the coffee table. From an envelope he extracted capsules and placed them beside the glasses.

"Please take your medicine, gentlemen," he said in his brisk, authoritative professional fashion, now a bit vitiated by a lisp. "It is not harmful, and in fact you are going to have a good rest for the next twenty-four hours."

"Now, look," the cop said. "This is—"

"I'm a druggist," Carter said. "I give you my word the dosage is harmless."

"Listen here," the cop said. "You don't want to commit a crime. Not people your age. Doing time would kill you. Think it over. I'm willing to forget I ever saw you, and so is Mr. Hoven, if you'll go out that door—"

"See the lady with the silencer on her piece, son?" Sam interrupted. "Would you like a real long sleep?"

"No," the cop said. "I'm not that dedicated to police work. That's what I was trying to say—like live and let live, see, and—"

"I'm getting tired of waiting," Sam said harshly.

Hoven seemed particularly horrified by Sid. "Why, she could be my mother," he said. "How could she—"

"You flatter yourself," Sid said. "And in a minute I'm going to let you have it."

"All right," the cop said. "But I warn you that you're breaking the law and everything you say or do may be used in evidence against you."

Paling, he swallowed his pills. Hoven's hands were shaking. He dropped a capsule on the carpet and had to retrieve it. When he swallowed, he gagged and coughed.

Hastening into the front bedroom, Sam returned

with pillow slips stripped from the beds. While Carter and Sid stood guard, he emptied the contents of the two cases in his improvised bags, of double thickness to withstand the weight; then he went to the bar and cleaned out the other cases. Gun hidden, he left by the front door, closing it behind him. Hoven and the policeman watched his exit blankly.

"Just for the record, Pop," the young man asked, "what did you give us?"

"Deserpidine," Carter said. "I won't tell you how many milligrams, but you have nothing to worry about. It is really not an overwhelming application."

"Never heard of it."

"What does it do to you?" Hoven said.

"Deserpidine relieves tensions," Carter explained. "Rids you of hidden aggressions. You'll have a feeling of euphoria, succeeded by drowsiness and complete relaxation."

"Why, that sounds attractive," Hoven said, and suddenly smiled; his unease and horror were leaving him. "I've been doing too much lately. Resort life is one continuous round of parties—all drinking, talking, staying up all night—and naturally in the daytime I have to practice the hard sell. Whatever you may see on the outside, Wycroft & Benz are actually the golden hand in the iron glove. You have to deliver when you're on a stiff expense account like mine . . . Am I rambling?"

"I find it very interesting," Carter said.

"I find you interesting, Pop," the cop said amiably. "You must lead an interesting life. How did you happen to get into this line of work? Was it late in life?"

"Rather late," Carter said. "I retired and needed something to keep me active, and the opportunities when you arrive at a certain age are pretty restricted."

"Yeah," the cop said. "Well, you got ability. This job has been well planned. Naturally I don't intend to butt in—I won't ask you where you're going with Mr. Hoven's stuff."

"Just out of town," Carter replied, and put away his gun; Sid was startled and didn't follow suit. "Permanently, my boy."

"What enchants me," Hoven said, "is that cute little elf, Mrs. Burton, with her revolver."

"Pistol," the cop said. "Automatic. And a silencer, baby." He yawned and covered his lips with a hand. "Pardon me."

"Yes," Hoven said. "Of course. If I don't drop dead —and that doesn't concern me terribly—I'm going to dine out on this amusing incident back East."

"I suppose your friend is already miles away with the stuff," the cop said approvingly. "Nice going, Pop. But don't let him forget you and your girl friend here later on."

"I'll remind him," Carter said.

"You forget I am Mrs. Burton," Sid said.

"Oh, yeah," the cop said. "Please excuse me, Mrs. Burton." He yawned again, blinked his eyes, and shook his head and grinned. "Listen, I'm the least hung-up I've ever been. This must be like the junk the kids are all taking. I feel as if I might get into my 'jammies— that's how my wife and I talk to the children—and sack out for a minute or two. Could you help me to the bedroom?"

"Certainly," Carter said, and moved over to give the young man a hand. Sid looked her alarm and trained her gun on them; Carter frowned in reproof and flinched.

The cop draped an arm around Carter's shoulders and was escorted to the front bedroom. "I've taken a liking to you, Pop," the cop said. "You remind me of my father. He runs a discount store in Palm Desert."

Highly concerned at what she regarded as Carter's recklessness and wondering whether she might be compelled to shoot both of them if the policeman attacked the frail old doctor, Sid followed, casting a quick eye back at Hoven, who was beginning to droop. Without incident, Carter assisted the cop in stretching himself on one of the twin beds and pulled a comforter up over him.

"Goodnight, Daddy," the cop said. "You couldn't have been nicer to me. I'll never forget you."

"Goodnight, my boy," Carter said. His voice grew incisive. "But you must forget us—every one of us. You have to do that for me. Do you understand?"

"Oh, sure," the cop said. "Whatever you say. But get your teeth fixed, huh? It spoils your looks."

"I hate to think we may never meet again, Mrs. Burton," Hoven said. "I admire you tremendously. Can't we keep in touch? I'm the soul of discretion—"

"No," Sid interrupted.

Carter came back to Hoven, giving Sid a hard glance in passing. She put away the pistol.

" 'Jammies," Hoven said. "What a dreadful term!" He laughed flutily. "But I'm afraid I'm ready for them. Will you both forgive me?"

"With pleasure," Carter said. "Why don't you curl up on the sofa? I'll put a pillow under your head and cover you—you'll be very comfortable."

"All right," Hoven replied. "Thank you so much. . . . Do you mind removing my sandals? My feet always swell when I lie down with anything on them."

Carter brought him a blanket and pillow from one of the bedrooms connecting with the right-hand hallway. He was gone for several minutes on the errand, and Hoven dozed. When he returned, he settled Hoven and removed his sandals.

"Bless you . . ." Hoven murmured, and sank into unconsciousness.

"Get Sam," Carter whispered.

After checking on the cop's slumber en route, Sid softly opened the front door. "Don't turn off the outside light," Carter hissed behind her. "It might attract attention." She dimly made out Sam crouched under the enveloping branches of a bottlebrush tree, his sacks at his side, and waved to him. Bringing his burdens, he scuttled into the house and she closed the door. Carter signaled them, and they followed him on tiptoe into the right hall.

"I managed to attract Brenda's attention and gave her the okay sign," Sam reported. "She jumped about two feet. There's practically no traffic on the street."

"I think I've found what we need," Carter said. "The master bedroom has a fireplace, but they have only a gas log in it—no wood is used. Underneath is a hole with a metal cover on it for dumping ashes when wood is burned. Come on."

He turned in a transverse hall, and Sam and Sid accompanied him to the large room on the front of the house where Hoven's calfskin luggage and possessions were neatly arranged. The small fireplace had a caramel-colored marble facing and ceramic log on an iron support, with a gas burner underneath. Kneeling, Carter employed a tool Sam gave him to carefully pry up a lid that plugged the square orifice. He raised his head questioningly.

"Well . . ." Sam said. It's obvious . . . easy to find."

"That's the advantage," Carter said. "We agreed we wouldn't dig a hole or get too cute."

"Won't the police go over the house inch by inch?" Sid asked.

"Why?" Carter said. "Didn't Hoven and the cop see Sam leaving with the stuff while they were still conscious? And why would robbers leave the jewelry at the scene of the crime?"

"We'll have to empty the sacks," Sam said. "They won't go down there intact."

"No matter," Carter said. "Look, we can't debate this, Sam. I say let's take the risk. If we have misjudged the intelligence of the police—and that is doubtful— then so be it."

"Okay," Sam said. "If they find it, at least they won't bother to hunt for us. Sid?"

"Okay," she said.

He emptied one sack and dropped the baubles from sight, and Sid and Carter unloaded the other. Sid paused, dazzled by violet shafts in her eyes.

"Oh my," she said. "That diamond necklace . . . I hate to see it go."

Carter removed it from her grasp. "No second thoughts, Mrs. Burton."

The contents of the second sack disappeared under the floor. Both sacks were shoved down. Sam replaced the metal cover and squatted closer to the bed of the fireplace.

"Turn on every light in the room," he said. "We've got to make absolutely sure we haven't left any evidence of somebody fooling around here."

Arising in a couple of minutes, he said he was satisfied. After the others had gone from the room, Carter had a last look about and turned off all the lamps, leaving it as he had found it.

They gathered in the living room. Hoven slept deeply, as did the cop; their faces were composed and cherubic. But the robbers had grown haggard. Accumulated strain and fatigue were taking a toll. Sid had to quell an impulse to weep tears of relief for their success.

"Well," she remarked. "This wasn't bad. . . ."

Carter smiled. "Our police friend complimented us, you'll recall."

"Uh-huh," Sam said. "Only we'd better congratulate each other after we're home. You go first, Doctor—you'll scare poor old Brenda less than one of us. Give us a wave if the street is clear."

Nodding, Carter advanced to the door. His hand was on the knob when they heard the sound of a car stopping, radio playing rock music loudly—and seconds later the roar of an engine and screeching tires as a second automobile plunged off leaving a wake of pounding, diminishing exhaust noise.

They could not immediately move or speak, paralyzed by shock and astonishment. The engine and radio of the first car were turned off, and a confused medley of loud voices arose.

"That was poor old Brenda taking off!" Sid breathed.

"Oh, boy," Sam said. His face was suddenly contorted with rage.

Carter gestured at the front bedroom, and they huddled together in there, backs to the supine cop. People approached the house, men and women, talking with the brassy assurance cocktails had given them.

"Hey," a man said, "who was the spooky colored lady in the Caddy? What's old Hank up to?"

"Simple enough," said a woman. "He's got a new nighttime companion. Henry's more of a swinger than we realized."

"She may not be black," a man said. "She might have just looked that way in the headlights. It may be a good tan. Give Hank the benefit of the doubt."

Everybody laughed.

"He's too old for romance," another man said. "And much too buttoned up. That was a maid."

"In a Cadillac?" a woman asked.

"Look," the man said, "this is Palm Springs."

"Well, we'll get to the bottom of it," a man said.

The chimes rang. "Hold tight," Carter whispered. "Perhaps they'll think Hoven's gone with his guard to put away his stock."

More chimes. "Hey, Henry Hoven!" a man yelled. "You've got company! Thirsty company. Open up!"

There were screeches and catcalls, and references to the dame Hank had been entertaining. A finger pressed uninterruptedly on the doorbell.

"Easy, easy," somebody said. "He's out stowing the crown jewels. We can wait."

Carter looked from Sam to Sid, compressing his

lower jaw until it nearly touched his nose. Sweat sprang up on Sam's forehead.

"I'm in need of a drink," a man said. "Hank gave me a spare key so I could stay with him tonight. I've got it here someplace . . ."

The lock turned. "We need room," Sam snapped. "Get ready. I'll do the talking."

"We could go through the rear—" Carter began.

"No," Sam said. "Not enough time. We might get trapped." He was shoving them out. "And Brenda may come back."

He closed the bedroom door behind them, and they moved apart to face the opening door. Four men and three women entered, bronzed and hearty and middle-aged, wearing colorful sports attire. "Hey, Hank," a man was saying, "the ship's sailed! Open the bar!"

The ingress stopped. Eyes widened at the trio and Hoven slumbering on the sofa. A silence fell.

"Good evening," Sam said. "I am Mr. Burton. This is my wife. That is Mr. Smithson."

"Oh?" a tall man said. "And that's Henry on the couch. What's the matter with him?"

"I can't imagine," Sam replied. "We're customers of his, and he was this way when we came. I suppose he's drunk."

"Yeah?" the tall man said. "He looks dead to me."

Someone gasped.

"Oh, no," Carter said. "I assure you he's breathing easily."

"If he was that way when you came," the tall man demanded, "how did you get in?"

"The door was open," Sam said. "We closed it and put on the lock for safety's sake."

"Sure, sure," the tall man said. He pointed to the open, empty morocco cases on the coffee table. "Do you mind explaining *them?*"

"Uh, shouldn't we be leaving, Mr. Burton?" Sid said.

"Yes, dear," Sam said. He managed to smile at the

assemblage. "I'm sure there must be some explanation for this, but we don't want to get involved. You're his friends. You can take care of Mr. Hoven."

"That we can, oldtimer," the tall man said. "But you're not leaving till we call the cops. Say! Wait a minute. Where's Jerry, his guard?"

"That's all," Sam said disgustedly, and produced his machine pistol and released the safety; Sid and Carter displayed their guns and made them ready—and Sid was distressed to find that despite Sam's training and admonitions she had been carrying a weapon with a very easy trigger pull wholly unsecured. "Everyone kneel and bend over, backs to me, hands under your heads."

"Now, look—" the tall man started to bluster.

Sam drew a bead on him. "One more word, you son of a bitch, and you get it. Mr. Smithson, cut the wires."

His orders were obeyed. Hurrying through the house, Carter ripped out the connections of three telephones. In spite of his enforced and menacing calm, Sid sensed that Sam shared her mounting panic and was by no means sure of what to do next; perspiration shone on his cheeks and forehead. Nor was Carter much steadier when he joined them, short of wind and scowling in his concentration. But he was thinking.

"Car keys," he said, with difficulty.

"Who has the keys?" Sam said instantly. "Throw 'em behind you."

No answer. No movement.

"I'm in a hurry," Sam said. "The next spread goes lower."

He fired a burst into the wall over the bent figures. It resembled the speeded-up and intensified clacking of a carpet-layer's hammer, and plaster flew and a picture shattered and fell on the floor. A woman cried out. The tall man fumbled in his pockets and tossed a key ring backward. Sid dived for it.

Sam flapped an elbow toward the door, and she ran and wrestled with the knob. Scuttling after her, Carter waited in the doorway for Sam to back up to him.

"I'm going to nail anybody who follows us," Sam said.

They lunged outside, Sam slammed the door, and they collided with one another running for the street. There stood a bulky station wagon. Sam whirled about. The front door was opening, and he loosed several rounds. Ricochets whined, wood splintered, the living room window disintegrated and dropped tinkling shards.

"You drive," Carter said to Sid. "Swing around and head toward the mountain."

She raced to the left side of the car and clawed her way under the wheel, grievously banging a knee on an obstruction. The instrument setup was unfamiliar and she couldn't find the ignition lock. Carter got in beside her, and Sam scrambled onto the seat behind.

"Don't turn on the lights," Carter said. He snatched the keys from her, put one in the ignition, and started the engine. "For God's sake, Sidney!" He lay half across her knees, head against the lower rim of the steering wheel, and released the parking brake. "Stomp on it!"

In the process of reversing direction, turning in a giddy arc with the tires howling, very uncertain of where she was going without headlamps, she had a flash of the street as far as the illuminated palm trees that lined both sides of Palm Canyon Drive four blocks away—and nothing moved between her and that main thoroughfare. Her heart rose, but she was all over the pavement and twice ran off in gravel and skidded perilously. Staring to the rear, Sam ordered her to put on the lights. She was unable to locate the switch. A car coming in the opposite direction blinked headlights in warning, momentarily blinding her. She hit a curb and bounced off. The other driver shouted, "Watch it, you crazy drunk!" in passing. Cursing, Carter leaned on her knees and pulled the correct knob.

"God-damn poor old Brenda forever," Sam said.

"Amen," Carter said.

They reached the dead end of a hilly street, the warning sign unseen by Sid, and she had to cramp the huge car around again.

"Wait," Sam said. "Cut the lights. Leave the engine running. Here's where we change."

On a rocky offshoot of the mountain above was an illumined house, but no habitation stood close to them. A dog barked, evidently at them, but in the distance, and grew silent when a man called and whistled to him.

Sam got out and divested himself of his disguise and outer garments and hat. He had spotted a gaping curbside opening for a storm drain, and into it he crammed his belongings. Sid and Carter did the same, and Sam ordered Carter to throw the cop's gun down the drain.

"Give me your pieces," he said. "I'm not going to part with them."

"No," Carter objected. "Lets get rid of them."

"No!" Sam said. "I might need a gun yet, even if you don't. And they're mine—they could be traced if found."

As he put their pistols into his shopping bag, Carter said: "What do we do now? Our plan is all shot to kingdom come."

"We split up," Sam said. "What else? You two go on foot and I'll try to find a place to hide the wagon. Remember the restaurant on Palm Canyon Drive with the line of people always in front of it?"

"Louise's?" Sid asked.

"Yes. Get in the line. We'll meet there and try to figure out what to do next. If you get caught, don't talk."

They began moving.

Taking deep breaths, aware of tremendous excitement and exertion, Sidney Ellen half ran toward the glow in the sky at the center of town. She was abysmally scared. The minutes elongated curiously. But she was alive and charged with a furious, self-protective energy; it was like being born again. She did not look back, even though she heard Sam driving the station wagon away, and she saw no more of Carter.

She covered two long blocks. Her legs were failing, her lungs bursting. A car was overhauling her. She moderated her pace. Headlights glared on her, and the car stopped. She sopped the sweat on her face with a handkerchief and turned with a chill spreading in her veins.

The driver, alone in the convertible with the top down, was a young man in an Edwardian suit and a dashing, wide-brimmed black hat. "Hi," he said. "What happened to your horse? Can I give you a lift?"

Somehow Sid repressed her hard breathing. "Yes, thank you. I outran the sheriff's posse, but my horse dropped dead."

"You look like Belle Starr," the young man said. "Where're you going?"

She got in beside him. He was from Evanston, Illinois, the car was rented, he was having a ball in the desert, and he was bound for a party in Cathedral City. She said she had been baby-sitting up the street, and the people couldn't take her home; she often walked like this. Impersonating a native, she gave him a variety of false information. He let her off downtown on Palm Canyon Drive, and she thanked him and recommended a good sunburn lotion. A boutique was open and she went in, found a size six light wool dress and matching coat that almost fitted, professed absolute admiration and no concern for unfashionable length, and bought them. The saleslady was pleased by her wanting to wear the garments immediately, sold her a funny little straw hat, and put her discarded clothing into a box. Sid left the establishment calmly, in good spirits.

Carter walked all the way, annoyed by his age and decrepitude. Nobody took notice of him, and he did

not see any police. He counted his pulse, wondering
how much longer it would be until he had a coronary,
and resolved to swear off saturated fats forever. However, it pleased him to note, with a physician's objec-
tivity, that he had not been badly frightened by the
mishap and had kept his head. The prospect of the
rigors ahead of him failed to induce panic. The possibility of imprisonment or death did not daunt him.
But when he thought of Brenda, instant symptoms of
severe hypertension alarmed him and made him unsure
of the future.

The house Sam selected appeared temporarily empty;
a lamp burned in the living room window, and the
light over the garage was on and the door raised. Nobody was on the street, and adjoining homes were
dark. He drove the station wagon slowly and quietly
into the garage, shut off the lights and engine, got out,
and lowered the door. Walking away, he was of the
opinion being an old man helped in certain situations.
He had endured a great deal and encountered many
vicissitudes in his life. Time dulled reaction and emo-
tion. Vintage blood ran slower. He felt quite sedate and
enormously, alertly capable.

Two blocks along a quiet, empty street his resolution
was put to the test. A black and white car with a high
radio aerial intersected his path at the corner; the
policeman, a middle-aged man, weary-faced, leaned
away from the wheel toward him. His manner had the
courtesy now enjoined upon police in troubled times;
still, he scrutinized Sam closely.

"Good evening, sir," he said. "Mind telling me
where you're going?"

"Sure thing," Sam said coolly. "To the goddam market. Because my goddam car broke down just after we
got in from L.A. The auto club doesn't answer, of
course. Like always, there's nothing to eat in the
house." He had caught a dim glimpse of a street sign.

"I live up on Via del Norte. Name's Forbes. You can't give me a ride, I suppose?"

"Why not? Get in."

Sam sat beside the cop, and they drove off. He put the shopping bag at his feet, and in indicating it managed to keep it open so he could seize a gun handily. "The first market you come to, officer. I like my own bag better—the sacks they give you in stores always split open when you're carrying canned goods."

The cop smiled. "Ain't it a fact?"

He looked tired, underpaid and getting along in years, and, surprisingly, Sam decided not to shoot him if anything went wrong; nobody liked the fuzz anymore, and it was just possible that they were more sinned against than sinning—anyhow, he was not going to add to their woes and resolved to surrender in an emergency. He felt warm and righteous. The cop glanced at Sam in a kindly fashion.

"Forbes you said your name was?" he asked. "Been in the neighborhood long? I don't seem to remember you."

"A couple of months. The swimming pool heater won't work. Coming here for weekends was my wife's idea. I wish I was back in L.A."

"Yeah. So do I. We lived in the Valley. My wife has asthma and had to try a dry climate. People move in and out of here all the time; it's hard to keep track of them. Somebody's always cleaning out the empty houses."

"They can have what we've got," Sam said. "The furniture came with our house and it all ought to go to the Salvation Army. Are you after someone?"

"Well, sort of. We had a blast from the dispatcher. A holdup. That's unusual."

"Holy smoke. I hope you don't run into 'em while I'm with you."

"Don't worry," the cop said. "Those guys are miles from here by now."

He stopped at a market, accepted Sam's thanks, and drove off talking into his microphone. Sam went into the market, bought bread and dishtowels to cover the guns (having casually put the shopping bag at a checker's stand with his hat over the contents) and left by a side entrance. At a hotel nearby he flagged a cab and rode to Louise's.

The line along the sidewalk in front of the restaurant was a long one, composed of jovial oldsters and teen-agers bent on eating slabs of cream pie. Sidney Ellen had to drop out once when she got too close to the entrance, walk around the block, and queue up at the end. Then she saw Sam coming along. He gave no evidence of recognizing her and joined the line several spaces back. Eventually she got inside and sat on a stool at the counter and ate a salad. Near her was Sam, eating pie and coffee. When she finished, she paid her check and lingered outside. Sam joined her.

"Where the devil is he?" he whispered. "They must have got him." He walked on. Sid overtook him. "Beat it, will you? We can't stay together."

"I was thinking," she said hurriedly. "They have commuter planes out of here—I phoned the airport. We can leave for San Diego in about an hour—"

"No. They'll be watching. And at the bus station."

Simultaneously they had the same thought. Sid spoke first: "Rent a car—"

"Good. You do it. I'll wait for Carter. If he doesn't show up in an hour we'll have to leave him." Sam consulted his watch. "Pick me up on the other main street, Indian Avenue, at eight o'clock—two blocks south—I'll be on a corner."

Suddenly they saw Carter approaching them on the sidewalk, hobbling a little, a black look on his face. Waving Sid off, Sam walked toward him.

A clerk in a drugstore directed Sidney Ellen to an imposing hotel; it had a car rental desk in the lobby.

She waited a few moments, considering. Sam feared the airport and bus station, but what about the car-hire agencies? There were many of them in a resort town, of course, and she saw no uniformed policemen around nor anyone in plain clothes who resembled a detective. Probably the most the cops would do was phone the agencies descriptions, and now those wouldn't match. Attempting to steal a car was too risky, even if she could manage it, and a quick stolen car report might get them caught before they reached San Diego. And the stubborn major was carrying the guns in his shopping bag. . . .

Wan, timid and smiling, Sid advanced to the desk. The helpful uniformed girl on duty paid no particular attention to her. She had to show her driving license, a necessary hazard.

"My husband and I have to go to dinner with friends at La Quinta," she explained. "Could you tell me how to get there? Oh, and when we finish our vacation we might want to visit my nephew in the Marine Corps at San Diego before we go home. Could we leave the car there?"

Yes. The agency had an office in San Diego; a small charge would be exacted for bringing the car back to Palm Springs. The girl supplied Sid with maps and detailed instructions. She started to breathe easier when a man brought the sedan to the hotel portico and pointed out the controls to her.

At eight P.M. she was heading south on Indian Avenue, having driven to all points of the compass and having made an important discovery. She discerned Sam on a corner and picked him up, and around the block picked up Carter, who sprawled on the rear seat, groaned, and said the arthritis had returned to his knees.

"Just to see," Sid said, "I drove farther south on the highway. The Highway Patrol's got a roadblock at the edge of Palm Desert. Before I turned off I could see them stopping everybody."

"Two dogs chased me," Carter continued. "One tried to bite me. Damn Brenda!"

Sam studied the map Sid gave him. "We'll go north first," he said, "until we hit an old road that parallels the freeway to Arizona. After we reach Indio, we'll circle back through the mountains. They can't cover everything."

"Oh, hell," Carter said exhaustedly. "By now they must have Brenda and know who to look for. She probably turned herself in or panicked and had a wreck."

In the early morning hours they reached San Diego, without incident. Sam had taken the wheel from Sid, and she had dozed fitfully. Awake after a long sleep on the rear seat, Carter was querulous and vindictive. The others could hear him creak as he straightened his cramped limbs.

"I'm an old man," he said, "not fitted for anything but retirement. This was all a mistake. I was too hasty and careless."

"In marrying," Sam gritted.

"Ah!" Carter said. "If Brenda is ever restored to me —if I can only have a moment alone with her—I'm going to give her an embolism with an empty hypodermic needle. So help me God!"

"I'll hold her for you," Sam said.

Sid wanted breakfast—her middle seemed to be caving in after a hard day and harder night—before they went to the motel on Mission Bay, the rendezvous where Biff Gagnon presumably awaited them; but Sam wouldn't hear of it.

"We've got to pick him up and go ahead with this as long as we can," he said. "There's a chance that goddam Brenda went home, and if she kept quiet we can work out another alibi. And we must not run the risk of keeping Biff waiting too long. He could turn into another Brenda with the pressure on."

He passed out the guns, saying they were for the possibility that everything had blown up and a reception committee of cops awaited them. It was almost a comfort for Sidney Ellen to again have the automatic that finished Mr. Jobal, but she felt sharp pains in her chest, of the kind warned about by the heart association.

The motel was huge. Rousing suddenly, grim and assured, with white stubble on his jaws, Carter went in the office to ascertain Biff's room number. Sam and Sid watched anxiously, thumbs on safety catches. Carter came back to them jauntily, nodding in reassurance, and they drove down a vast parking lot and parked at the proper number.

A reddish, moistly comfortable dawn embraced them. To the left of their rental sedan stood Dr. Tilden's Cadillac, license plates restored. They looked first in disbelief, and then triumphantly.

"Good old Brenda . . ." Sid said.

"I just couldn't help it," Brenda said. "They came tearing up behind me, and there were so many of them, and—and I got scared to death. . . . After I beat it, I was afraid to come back. But I stopped at a service station and bought gas and asked the man to put on my new plates for me—I told him I'd been carrying them around for days."

Leaning over, Carter kissed her cheek. "That's all right, my dear."

Brenda fought back tears. "Carty, I'm so glad you're not mad at me. All I could think of was meeting Biff and maybe hearing that you'd got away."

"I told her there was nothing to worry about," Biff said. He got up to pull the window shades and nearly knocked over a chair; his complexion, usually ruddy, was a saffron color.

"You did not," Brenda said. "You wanted to leave

and I wouldn't let you. Anyway, where would you have gone?"

"Wait a minute," Biff said. "I only suggested we drive around for a while and think things over."

"Never mind," Sam said, and contemplated Biff with squinty eyes. "Call the coffee shop. If it's open, we'll have breakfast."

They made a genial quintet in the coffee shop, enjoying their ham and eggs and waffles and conversation—typical retired, elderly tourists, rather loud and exuberant. When the meal was over and they had returned to Biff's room he was dispatched with the rental sedan to the local agency.

"You're Mr. Buckner," Sid reminded him. "I signed up as Mrs. Buckner. Don't get flustered if there are any questions."

Although he smiled, Biff had an uncertain air to him and his yellowish hue had not entirely disappeared. Sam watched his exit glumly.

"There goes the second-weakest link in our chain," he said.

"I guess I'm first," Brenda said. "Well, you can have your old chain. Do you realize I sacrificed my reputation last night?"

"Yes," Sam told her. "By running. You're a coward."

"That isn't what I mean! I had to stay here all night with Biff. He registered as a single. The desk clerk and the maids probably think I'm having an affair."

"With Biff?" Sid asked. "You must be joking, Brenda."

"We sat up, and I even wore my coat, and I hate to say anything in front of Carty, who'll be furious, but Biff said a couple of things to me that might surprise you if I were unladylike enough to repeat them—which I am not."

"I am *not* furious," Carter said. "I'm completely uninterested in your sacrifice, and I share Sid's opinion that Biff is harmless."

Brenda grew red. "Very well. I'm sorry I mentioned it. But I kept him here, didn't I? Don't think he wasn't ready to run out on you!"

"Yes, dear. Thank you. We're all grateful, and proud of you."

She was mollified. "That's better. . . . Carty, will you do something for me?"

"Gladly."

"Promise me you'll never do anything like this again."

"I promise."

"Well," she said. "That's more like it."

"This was insufficiently studied and organized," he said. "We were lucky to get by with it—and we still have no real assurance of a payoff. Next time we'll have a better proposition."

"Oh, my God!" she cried.

Biff returned promptly, in high spirits and exuding relief. Disposing of the car had been a routine transaction, no questions asked. "You should have seen me as Mr. Buckner," he said, and winked suggestively at Sidney Ellen. "It just came naturally, kid."

"We still have a hundred thousand dollars to collect," Carter said.

"Let's enjoy ourselves instead of talking business," Sam said. "Why don't we go to the zoo or that place where they have all the marine animals? I wouldn't mind having a couple of martinis at lunch. When we get back to Golden Years, we'll tell everybody we had such a wonderful time that we had trouble breaking away."

As proof of his improved state of mind, he allowed the shopping bag to be locked in the trunk. His companions brightened noticeably at that.

Biff retrieved his eroded reputation in the National Guardian negotiations. But first two weeks were allowed to elapse. The Palm Springs jewel robbery achieved a brief and flattering glory in the press and the other media. The circumstances of elderly bandits, one of them female, and the victims being drugged (both Henry Hoven and his guard recovered from their sleep nicely, and found themselves greatly refreshed) attracted considerable attention. Naturally Hoven exaggerated his loss, which he put at half a million. One headline read: JEWELER AND GUARD DRUGGED; ROBBERS ESCAPE IN HAIL OF BULLETS; another: GRANDMA BANDIT HEADS HALF MILLION JEWEL CAPER. Television had filmed interviews featuring Hoven, his guard, a man from the second group which had surprised the robbers, and some pained policemen. The policemen said it was obviously the job of professionals and seemed unsettled at the thought of old people joining everyone else in the commission of crimes. It was next day before the garaged station wagon was reported, and police theorized that the three holdup artists were picked up later by their getaway car (a note of piquancy was added up later by the fact that it was a new Cadillac) and made a clean escape. But they added that the jewelry was too valuable to be easily disposed of and they expected arrests shortly. The integrated character of the operation was duly noted, and a hunt was on for the colored woman serving as wheelman for the gang. The Guardian National Insurance Company offered a ten-thousand-dollar reward for information leading to recovery of the jewelry and the arrest and conviction of the robbers, an offer so hedged and complicated that almost no one could understand the terms. After a few days everybody forgot about it. Someone was always getting knocked over in Palm Springs during the winter season.

Then Biff called Guardian's home office in New York from a pay station in Pasadena. He intrigued an underling and eventually talked to a vice-president named Cyril P. Loughner, whom he had heard of but did not know. "How bad do you want the Wycroft & Benz stuff back?" he asked.

"Well, pretty badly," Cyril P. Loughner said. "Who are you?"

"Never mind. How are the police doing on the case?"

"Why should I tell you?"

"I'll tell you why," Biff said. "Because unless you play footsie with me, the jewelry's going down the drain—nobody will ever see it again and you'll have to pay off in full. That was the whole object of this raid—for you to ransom it, see—that and nothing else."

"Oh . . . well, the police have some leads. Several people looked at the house before the robbery, perhaps casing it, and they're running them down. And they hope to find the Cadillac. We have a man from a private detective agency checking on it for us."

"Believe me, Mr. Loughner, you can cream this deal by holding out on me. Are they getting anywhere? If so, the stuff is going to disappear forever."

"Well, no, they aren't. Now, wait a minute, whoever you are. I wouldn't lie to you."

"Good," Biff said. "I want a hundred thousand for returning the jewelry. You get every piece back."

"A hundred thousand! I can't—"

"Okay. I'll mail you a tape recording of the toilet flushing."

"Wait a minute. Why, I'd have to take this up with the board of directors. And how do I know you—"

"Mr. Loughner, you know. You and I are both crooks, except you have a more legitimate front than I have, and you realize the stuff is worth nothing to me. All I want is your payoff."

"Send me one small piece to prove you have it."

"Sorry."

They wrangled. Eventually Loughner agreed to take

up the matter with the board. He wanted to know how he could get back to his caller.

"You can't," Biff said. "I'll check in with you in a couple of days. By the way, I'm phoning from pay stations in different towns—you needn't bother trying to trace the calls."

He was confident of being on firm ground, and he liked the process of negotiating. The jewelry was evidently safely hidden, and there seemed no prospect of an intensive search of the house since both Hoven and the cop had seen Sam leave with the loot in the pillowcases, presumably to turn it over to the accomplice in the Cadillac. That the cops were investigating people taken by real estate agents to the house was a little worrisome, but since Biff had given a false name and address, had no police record, and didn't intend to go to Palm Springs again he thought the chances of his getting picked up didn't amount to much. He felt he could safely assume the hippies on the motorcycles would never think of going to the police about the Cadillac they had seen in a totally different location and he was sure the kid the task force had encountered had long since forgotten the episode.

Biff waited five days to renew contact with Loughner, presuming he would be on pins and needles by that time. He was; Biff's lack of haste evidently lent credibility to his demands. From a phone booth in Claremont he did considerable dickering. Loughner said that the board would pay if Loughner was willing to accept responsibility for the deal and its successful outcome, but that they refused to go over fifty thousand. The stuff wasn't even worth two hundred thousand—Hoven had lied in giving the value of the jewelry, and Wycroft & Benz was trying to stick Guardian.

"That figures," Biff said. "We're all thieves. But it's still a hundred or the rocks go into the sewer."

"For God's sake," Loughner pleaded, "give me a

break. I'm taking you on trust, am I not? What solid proof have I that you've got the stuff? Listen, my head is on the block if you don't deliver."

To reassure him, Biff recounted each step of the robbery up to the gang's departure (he mentioned that the getaway car rescued them after they stashed the station wagon at a prearranged emergency gathering place), and described minutely the individual appearances of the robbers and the house. Sounding less uncertain, Loughner resumed bargaining.

"Look, I can't go back to my associates with an offer of fifty," Biff said. "You got to go higher."

"Sixty. That's tops."

"Ninety, you mean."

"Sixty-five. I tell you the board—"

"Eighty."

"Seventy."

Biff settled at seventy-five; he simply could not pull Loughner above that figure. "I'll try it out on them, Loughner. I don't think they'll take it."

"Aren't you the mastermind? Didn't you plan this, don't you run the mob?"

"Why, you might say that." In a way, Biff thought, he *was* the top banana.

"Well then, put your foot down. Close the deal. I swear I'm exceeding my authority in giving you seventy-five. You're murdering me!"

"Don't get emotional. I'll submit your bid and get back to you."

"Please, please, don't keep me waiting," Loughner said. "The board thinks I'm crazy, and Wycroft & Benz is pressuring us for payment. I'm risking my career in dealing with you."

Biff presented the offer to his friends. There was no question of acceptance, and he was thanked and complimented. But he allowed Loughner to sweat for a while. When, in Seal Beach, he called New York, he was put through promptly. "You didn't hurry," Loughner said bitterly. "Well?"

"I'm ready to close."

"All right, but I must be out of my mind. . . . How do you want the money?" Loughner paused significantly. "In what denominations, and where do we pay?"

"And with the serial numbers all copied down?"

"I promise I won't keep a record of the money."

"Sure you won't," Biff said, and laughed. "You needn't bother with cash. I'll accept a check."

"Huh?"

"Listen to me carefully. Make out one of your standard claim checks. Leave the payee's line empty—we'll fill it in. Address an envelope enclosing the check to Mrs. Milton McKenzie, General Delivery, Murrieta, California. Allow ten days for the pickup and another twenty days for the check to clear. Then you'll get your stuff."

Loughner stuttered: "A-a ch-check? What'll they think of next?" He seemed to rouse himself. "Look, I can't do that. The check might get lost, and somebody else could fill in a name and collect. And I can't wait twenty days for—"

"Okay. End of deal."

"Wait a minute. When I pay you, I want the jewelry—"

"Too bad."

"Wait! Can't you see my side of it? You're asking me to pay without the slightest assurance that you'll deliver. What's to keep you from holding out on me when you've got the money?"

"It's very simple," Biff said. "Why should we keep the stuff after we've been paid? What the hell would we do with it? Besides, we want to establish good relations with you; we may be doing more business in the future."

Loughner groaned. "Not that. Try somebody else."

"Keep on listening to me, Mr. Loughner. Mrs. McKenzie will come to pick up the check. I don't say when. Murrieta is a one-horse town, and the post office is a separate building. If anybody else is around—a single stranger—she won't make the collection. Don't plant any cops or investigators or you'll queer the deal. Somebody will be watching her and the pickup. If the least thing goes wrong, I can promise you the jewelry disappears for keeps a few minutes later. You may find out who took the stuff, but you'll still settle in full with the insurant. Get it?"

"Yes. Have you ever been in the insurance business, by any chance?"

"Me?" Biff said. "No. But I'm in a crooked line of work same as you. It all washes out, huh?"

Sidney Ellen was selected for the collection job, which constituted an honor; it could be rough. Aided by Bill, she equipped herself with a snood, dark glasses, thick eyebrows, pale makeup, a red rinse on her hair. She drove a rented car. Sam followed her in another rented car. He gave her the silenced automatic to put in the capacious handbag she carried.

Murrieta was a hamlet, selected and studied by Carter beforehand. He specified an arrival at exactly 1:30 P.M., a time when surrounding natives were either having a nap or working in the fields. Sam and Sidney Ellen were fully briefed. Six days had now elapsed since Biff had been in communication with Mr. Loughner.

They drove into town on the dot. The new, small post office, a recent pork barrel gift to the community, lay set aside on a large lot. Nobody stirred on the main street. Sidney Ellen could see inside the post office, and the only occupant was the man behind the counter. He did not react to the name of Mrs. Milton McKenzie when she went to the counter, nor apparently think it odd that she kept her handbag open, and handed over the letter.

In no hurry, Sid used a forefinger to slit the envelope. "Oh, how nice," she said. "I had a loss a while ago—some burglars got into my place—and the insurance company promised to pay." There was the check, payee unnamed, in the amount of seventy-five thousand dollars. "Gee! They gave me more than I expected."

"I'm glad to meet somebody that got something from an insurance company," the man said. "No one has ever got anything around here unless they died. Are you new, Mrs. McKenzie? I haven't seen you before."

"I'm staying at Kamp Karefree, the guest ranch," Sid said. "I'm a widow, and I was so upset when I found what the burglars had done that I had to get away."

"Well, enjoy yourself," the man said. "We got a beautiful valley here."

"Just lovely," Sid said. "I'm enjoying every minute away from Glendale."

She put the envelope in her purse and left her hand inside, grasping the gun; then she strolled outside. Across the street, the engine of his car running, was Sam, ready to cover her exit with the machine pistol.

Making several eccentric turns on lanes and byways, Sid went back to a car rental agency in Santa Ana, Sam following a quarter of a mile behind her. They were completely undisturbed, which Biff had predicted. He said insurance companies were reliable only when dirty work was involved, that some honor existed among thieves, and all you needed to do was get mixed up with the right people.

Dr. Tilden filled in the serial number of his Swiss bank account on the payee's line of the check with a typewriter, made a nameless endorsement on the reverse side paying only to the account, and sent it off to Anton Grundich et Cie Bank, Zurich, by air mail. Long before he had established the connection in order to funnel off tax-free cash payments from patients, a common practice in his profession.

"It helps to get an early start in cheating," he commented, and permitted himself a wintry smile. Perhaps insisting on cash on the line hinders a lot of criminal enterprises. Working through regular channels gives confidence and is more dignified."

Biff phoned New York from Port Hueneme. It was a moment of triumph, and he had never felt better in his life. He thought he had at last found his metier, just as he had decades before as a fullback. And Loughner was thunderstruck when Biff told him where the stuff was. Oddly, he stammered his thanks—such was the simplicity of it, that he believed every word.

"Those goddam stupid cops!" he said. "And Hoven! I'll get the son of a bitch fired!"

"Let's be broadminded, Loughner," Biff said graciously. Even the major had told him that he had appraised the situation and handled the negotiations beautifully, and that they needed him; he now considered himself the brains of the combine. They often characterized athletes as all brawn and no brain, but they didn't take into account the latter stages of their careers. "What you have on a typical police force is a bunch of guys with strong backs and not much initiative. Except for luck, they might have been inside the jail instead of guarding it. Give them credit for trying."

"I've seen the canceled check from Switzerland. Don't think we won't follow that up."

"Go ahead. Others have tried. Why do you think the Swiss encourage every crook in the world? Can you suggest a better arrangement?"

"No," Loughner said. "And somehow, God help me, I believe we'll find the jewelry where you said. You don't miss anything, do you?"

"Why, I believe I can say I have my finger on the button," Biff told him.

The cops removed the jewelry from under the fire-place. They had a hard time explaining the lapse in thorough procedures. The "Grandma Bandit" had more exposure in the media: A Guardian National spokes-man explained that unnamed informants had led to disclosure of the cache, then accepted congratulations. He said apprehension of the robbers was momen-tarily expected. Henry Hoven got fired by Wycroft & Benz.

"Seventy-five thousand . . ." Brenda said. "All that money in Carty's name! Gee whiz! What are we going to do next?"

THERE WAS A LAPSE in the unlawful activities of the Golden Years group. Nothing presented itself, in fact, and the advent of spring and early summer doldrums inhibited action.

They permitted themselves a discreet affluence, drawing on Dr. Tilden for modest sums. Sidney Ellen traded in her old Chevrolet and bought one of the smaller Buicks—of course on a time payment plan. The dealer was a trifle concerned by her financial situation, but she took pleasure in earnestly assuring him that she could pay for the car.

Bill Canary bought bibelots and prints for his trailer, and a leopard skin for the floor. Success permitted Biff to play for somewhat higher stakes in golf, shuffleboard and gin rummy, and with less desperate concentration. Carter and Brenda flew off for a vacation in Victoria, British Columbia. The major added a new lathe to his garage workshop.

But when the Tildens came home and summer was in full swing, everybody was a bit restless.

Again Biff Gagnon suggested a caper, the word they had borrowed from the newspaper description of their Palm Springs debut. This one had the disadvantage of being uncomfortably close to their base, but the possibilities were intriguing.

Biff had played golf several times with a man named

Grover T. Gaston, a dreadful old boy formerly an automobile dealer in Southern California at several locations. He specialized in the sale of used cars. The advent of television advertising in the late Forties had made him rich and notorious (he appeared before the camera himself and gave fervid spiels), and his unorthodox business practices had resulted in many suits and an investigation by the state attorney general which compelled him to sell out to avoid prosecution.

Now, vigor apparently unimpaired, he was retired. Although not a resident of Golden Years, he had numerous friends in the colony and was often a guest at the Snug Harbor country club, where he was regarded as the terror of the greens, the bar, the lounge and the dining room. Several members had written stiff letters to the executive committee demanding that he be barred, but so far no action had been taken. A tall, thin, rubbery-nosed, flabby-lipped, white-haired man, once an attorney specializing in accident cases and once married to a wealthy woman who divorced him after being mulcted of much of her money, Gaston was loud, overbearing, conceited, drunken and lecherous—and almost always a winner at golf for stakes even the Snug Harbor people blanched at. He did his drinking only at the nineteenth hole and afterward insulted other senior citizens, as well as telling filthy jokes and pinching their wives and making improper proposals to them. His current home was a sixty-foot power cruiser moored at a private marina south of Long Beach, and gossip had it that he was forever entertaining women there; this was confirmed by his own bragging.

"Really?" Sam asked. "How old is he?"

"Well, pushing seventy anyhow," Biff said.

"What does he do with them?"

"Your guess is as good as mine. But a lot of old guys—" Biff looked suddenly at Sid—"I'm not taking any bows, see—are perfectly able to—"

"Let's not get into the clinical aspects," Carter interrupted. "He sounds as if Sid ought to kill him, but that's not what you're getting at, is it?"

"No," Biff said. "He putts like a pro when the chips are down, but he didn't beat me. That made him sore. We had a return match and I took him again. Steam came out of his ears. Afterward he wouldn't play me, or even say hello, and I had to push him to settle. He gave me a check he stopped payment on. When I squawked he insulted me and said gambling debts are not collectible under the law. I had to give up on the louse."

"Surely, muscleman," Bill said, "you're not proposing we collect for you?"

"Hell, no. Here's the angle: the other night I was in the bar at the club and overheard Grover loudmouthing to his pals nearby. He was smashed as usual. The subject was taxes and the damn government; it always is in the club. Grover winked at them and said if you were reasonably bright you didn't have to tell everything you knew, or keep a record of everything. Liquid assets were the solution. You never heard him complaining. Somebody questioned him, and I think he got a little spooked. 'Listen,' he said, "you're not getting anything from me. You think I'm bucking for another investigation? But I'll give you suckers a little hint. Use good old-fashioned methods—bury the stuff in your backyard, or put it somewhere safe. The hell with interest or dividends you pay taxes on. Tax-free principal is enough. How you get it in the first place, though, is your problem." Then he changed the subject and suggested another guy buy a round of drinks."

"Grover . . ." Brenda said. "Oh, yes. He's just awful. He's put his hand on my behind at the club, and what he said to me I won't repeat; as a lady, I couldn't. I didn't dare tell Carty."

"And you needn't bother now," Carter told her. "Go on, Biff."

"Well, suddenly I remembered something I'd read about his divorce a few years ago. His wife sued him for recovery of the money she'd let him have, as well as alimony. She claimed he ran around with other dames all the time and that he was concealing community assets. She demanded an inspection of a safe deposit box he had at the Frontier National Bank—the bum check he gave me reminded me of the name—which she said was full of cash he hadn't paid taxes on."

Sid leaned forward. "How much?"

"Two or three hundred thousand, but she was trying to nail him; I suppose she exaggerated. I don't believe she got anywhere with it. He had the best lawyers in town representing him."

"Frontier has lots of branches," Sam said. "Which one is supposed to have the money?"

"I don't know," Biff said. "It shouldn't be hard to find out, though. And I'll tell you this: he's one of the few guys left who wears an old-time repeater watch the size of a turnip and a chain, and on the chain is a fob and a key that looks like it's for a bank box. I've seen it when he has been looking at the time. Wouldn't that be the one?"

"Perhaps," Carter said. "What else?"

"That's all. I have no idea of how we dip into Grover's till. It was only an idea."

"Biff, you ought to be with the Central Intelligence Agency," Bill remarked sourly.

"Yeah? Remember Palm Springs. That didn't sound so good at first either, did it?"

"Impossible." Carter paused. "Except that I've met Gaston. He's overdue. . . ."

The very intangibles beckoned to them. It should never be too easy, Carter observed, and to know a man you wouldn't buy a used car from was to hate him. They did some preliminary work. Biff was adept at masked inquiries, and he soon established Grover's ghastly character and murky background. The existence of a treasure trove of illegal banknotes belonging

[70]

to Grover seemed to be common knowledge; while in his cups over the years, he had evidently talked a great deal. How much he had, naturally, was pure speculation. Still, nobody thought the old thief had stashed away less than a couple of hundred thousand.

Representing herself as a secretary in a yacht brokerage firm, Sid telephoned the Yachtsmen's branch of the Frontier National Bank in quest of credit information on Mr. Gaston, and talked to the assistant manager. Mr. Gaston was, she said, considering the purchase of a rather large boat from her firm and a question of his financial responsibility had arisen. This was all confidential, of course, and she had been told to make sure no word of the inquiry got back to Mr. Gaston; the salesman said he was a pretty touchy man.

The assistant manager, a Mr. Cooper, laughed and said: "Oh, I'll keep your secret, Miss Sommers. And I don't mind giving you a little general information. Mr. Gaston has a reputation for hard dealing, but I can assure you he is highly solvent. We have had his accounts for several years, and although he presents some difficulties as a customer, we find him on the whole quite reliable."

"You handle all his banking matters, sir?"

"Yes. He uses our full range of services and deals with us exclusively. But I wouldn't advise your firm to take this matter too seriously. Mr. Gaston is always looking at ocean-going yachts and planning a cruise around the world, but he never gets any farther than the first stages."

It was apparent from Cooper's tone of voice that he, like everyone else, detested Grover. On hearsay, Sidney Ellen began to despise him herself and to favor the project. Nevertheless, sheer animus was not sufficient for putting together an intelligent crime. Even when the group was reasonably sure of the validity and location of the hoard, no method of getting at it seemed feasible. Kidnapping and torture were considered, but everything in that line was far too complicated and risky. Their interest started to wane when nobody came up with a suitable alternative.

Then one night while they were having a nightcap at Sam's house after an appallingly dull square dance at the Sunset Town community center, he said casually, "I've been thinking over the Grover thing. It's simple. We bust open the bank."

They were surprised, and yet the advantages he enumerated had the ring of splendid simplicity. If they opened and looted Grover's box, he would not be able to report his loss. Bashing in a safe-deposit vault was, Sam had taken the trouble to learn, easier than opening a money vault—the armoring wasn't usually so heavy. They would go well equipped, and if Grover didn't have the assets claimed or had too small an amount, they would rob the bank.

"Hold on," Carter said. "How do we determine whether Grover *has* a box at the Yachtsmen's branch and what the number is? Sid didn't definitely find that out, and you wouldn't have the time or strength to open every—"

"Correct," Sam cut in. "That's a preliminary step. We verify Biff's assumption that Grover has a key, get a wax impression of it, and I make a duplicate."

"And how do we go about that?"

"Grover has uninvited guests on his boat. They rob him and lift his watch, but they don't bother to take his key."

"You're forgetting something," Bill said. "It requires two keys. The girl who takes you in the vault always has to use her key, too."

"Right. But she doesn't take the key home with her, does she? Where is it kept after hours?"

"I'll look into that for you," Biff said. "I love the idea of robbing the bastard. Couldn't you shoot him?"

"Only if necessary," Carter said. "This is a fail-safe situation: we take care of Grover, and then determine whether to go forward. Meanwhile we must do some thorough research."

"A bank!" Brenda said. "My God, Carty! Im going to get a divorce."

"I'm all for it," Carter replied. "But for obvious reasons, this is like the Mafia. Once you're in, you stay in —until death do you part."

Every eye was on Brenda. She paled, and put a hand to her throat.

Accompanied by his wife, Carter explored the Mooreea Marina. It looked attractive in his Polaroid color shots. Over a hundred boats of varying sizes lay in their slips at the lagoon, nearly surrounded by an exotic, palm-tree-fringed fill and breakwater, and there was a clubhouse, living quarters for rent, repair and fueling facilities, and a parking lot. The doctor noted, in the course of several visits, that it was a hive of activity on weekends but comparatively deserted otherwise, especially in the late-night hours. A watchman of antique brand made his rounds after dark, but they were desultory. Helped by a bystander, Carter identified Grover's craft, an imposing cruiser with a flying bridge called *Bounty II*. Grover was one of relatively few owners who lived aboard; these boats, generally of greater dimensions, were accommodated at the moorings farthest from shore in the deeper water and hooked up to telephone, power and water lines. They were removed from the general activity. The Mooreea management furnished a cleaning service which operated on Mondays. Carter's informant, voluble and well informed about the habits of the *Bounty II* skipper, spoke enviously of the many callers he had, mainly at odd times —it was the talk of the marina, and old Grover had exacted a grudging respect from gossipers.

Next Carter investigated the Yachtsmen's branch of the Frontier National Bank. Frontier had reason to be proud of its newest addition, situated not far from

Mooreea and adjacent to a small business section. The building, out on a spit of land and overlooking a rocky shoreline, did not resemble a conventional bank. It was well removed from other structures, prefaced by considerable lawns and semitropical planting, and circular in shape. Walls of the single story were of solid glass from floor to ceiling, heavily tinted to mitigate the glare of the sun. All functional equipment, vaults and employee space were concentrated in the center, the remainder being left clear for patrons. At night, with lights left on, it resembled a kind of amber beacon visible at sea.

Through his sources, Biff amplified Carter's findings. Insurance companies knew everything, and he had little difficulty in getting vital details from Frontier's insurer. The branch was well equipped with electronic warning devices inside and out, and a direct alarm line ran to the nearest cops. No guard was on duty daytimes, and no night watchman paid visits, although the outfit that installed and maintained the security equipment had people who made occasional checks when the branch was closed.

"It's funny," Biff said. "Banks are strong for solid business practices and getting the last buck out of the borrower and not taking any chances, but they hate to spend a penny on anything. Take these new offices they have, which look like the last word in modern living. You know what the secret is? The money goes into computers and getting rid of low-paid clerks, but not into something that resembles a bank. The Yachtsmen's branch is a good example. Frontier built it for peanuts, relatively speaking—it's all show. I talked to the construction company that does their work. They had a weight and space problem and everything was skimped. There's only five inches of concrete laced with steel mesh on the vault and strong room instead of the usual ten to fifteen inches that has steel alloy plates bolted on the inside. You could probably open either one of them with a diamond drill and a blowtorch. More money was spent on soundproofing and air conditioning than anything else. Of course, Frontier's argument is that nobody would try to open a joint which is totally exposed. And they have a point, huh?" He appeared a little dashed.

"Maybe not," Sam said. "You mentioned you'd discover where the safe-deposit clerk puts her keys. Did you?"

"Sure. Do I ever fail you? I have a copy of the standard security regulations for the Frontier home bank and all branches. The keys go in a drawer so marked in the safe-deposit vault every night; the vault is protected by the same time-lock steel doors as the strong room, and both have barred grilles which have to be unlocked by keys the manager and his assistant carry."

"You're invaluable, Biff," Carter said. "But how careful are you? Have you been identified with these inquiries?"

"Nope. My conversations have been by phone, and I represent some New York underwriters who never heard of me. I even changed my voice when I talked of how we were considering buying a piece of the bank action out here."

"Wonderful. You are our mainstay."

"Well," Biff said. "Thank you. I do my best. But I can't help you on the alarm system. It's as good as they come, with five or six different circuits and all sorts of backups. I think they have us."

"You're mistaken," Sam said.

He went to study the Yachtsmen's branch and to check on a minor hindrance Carter had noted at the marina, a locked gate at the entrance to the slips which was opened by keys supplied only to boat owners. At the next meeting, he said: "Soundproofing and the opaque windows will work to our advantage in the bank. I have an idea or two I'll explain later, and I've got to do a little welding in my garage. The gate at

Mooreea is no problem—it's merely a spring lock, not a dead bolt, and I can open it with a stiff sheet of plastic. Breaching the walls of the vault is a cinch."

"And the alarm system?" Carter asked.

"I can solve that for you," Sam replied, "and we can have some fun besides. My vote is to proceed on the first phase."

Everybody voted in accordance with him except Brenda, who stated that she was no bank robber.

"Correct," Sam said. "You have another function."

"Oh," Brenda said. "That's different."

On the appointed night, the group assembled at Dr. Tilden's, ostensibly for bridge. Biff was very late in arriving; he had been engaged in obtaining a rental sedan in Los Angeles and watching activities at Mooreea. By then preparations were well advanced. In loose sweater and slacks, face heavily made up and equipped with thick eyebrows and pouches under her eyes, a pistol, a small bottle of chloroform and absorbent cotton in her purse, Sidney Ellen was ready. Beside her was a slight girl, curvy, curly-haired, in a print dress and light coat, with painted nails and high-heeled slippers and mod figured stockings. It was Bill, and he seemed to relish his transformation. He also had a gun in his handbag, and a leather-covered sap furnished by Sam. His earnest solicitations had secured him the job, not to mention his offer to change sex for the occasion. There had been some politely expressed doubts about his suitability. Carter had abruptly quashed objections, saying, "We all have to participate, and it's time Bill got his feet wet. He's our man. Or woman."

"Thank you, luv," Bill had said. "I can do anything in drag I can do otherwise."

After paying his taxi driver, Biff hastened inside. He stared at Bill and came to a stop. "Baby, you do something to me," he said.

"Oh, kiss my ass," Bill said.

"That's enough!" Carter snapped.

"Sorry," Biff said. "Grover was aboard, as of when I left the marina half an hour ago. I think he had dinner at the clubhouse. I can almost guarantee he's alone." He handed Sid a parking check. "The car's in the parking lot at the Long Beach Municipal Auditorium. It's a sixty-nine Ford. I wrote the license number on this paper. Fourth row on your left."

"Make the last check, Sid," Sam commanded.

She sat down at the telephone and did her practiced mimicry of a long-distance operator. Grover T. Gaston answered and identified himself. He profanely refused to accept a long-distance call collect from Amarillo, Texas, and said he had never heard of a Fred Means. "I never take collect calls," he said. "Operator, what do you mean by calling me at nearly eleven o'clock? You got me out of bed. Get the hell off the goddam line!"

Sid got up. "He's there—and being nasty."

"All right," Carter said. "I'll signal you from outside."

"Lots of luck, girls," Biff said, and grinned.

Apparently inspecting his front garden, Carter ascertained that things were quiet in Snug Harbor and gave a sign. Sid and Bill went out, got into Sid's new Buick, and drove away. Carter stood with his hands behind his back, contemplating another peaceful night.

Sidney Ellen parked her car in a lot a block from the auditorium, and she and Bill walked to the entrance, where a cat fanciers' show was in progress; then they went to the adjacent parking lot and found the Ford. A young attendant smiled at Bill as they departed, and he smiled back.

He and Sid had been lavishly instructed and had made trial runs, chauffered by Brenda, that day and the day before—so finding the marina was easy. The parking area was only partially filled. In a lighted sentry box sort of office at the entrance sat an elderly man in a blue uniform and cap with a telephone on his desk; he waved to them abstractedly, and Bill returned the wave. According to Carter's information, the watchman rarely began his tours before midnight and he always kept his flashlight pointed downward because of complaints of boat owners deep in amours or sleep.

Sid reversed the car between two white lines near the steps leading down to the moorings, leaving the nose pointing out. Lighting was adequate at Mooreea, but not overpowering. She sat for a moment looking around. No one was visible but the man in his distant sentry box. Then she got out and led the way to the gate in the shoreline chain-link fence. Again she paused, Bill dutifully at her side. Faint sounds of music and voices came from the clubhouse. Water lapped on the wooden floats, and the boats in them moved softly, creaking and rubbing hulls on padded canvas buffers and old auto tires. All the mooring walkways were deserted, and just two craft showed interior illumination; both were on the outermost line where Sid and Bill were bound.

Upon Sid's gesture, Bill produced the thin strip of plastic Sam had given him, fiddled briefly with the lock, and the gate opened. They headed for the deep-water slips. Despite their speed and the uneven, unsteady footing, Sid noted approvingly that Bill did not once stumble in his spike heels.

Bounty II was unlighted. Sid barely hesitated before mounting the little gangway. She and Bill had pored over plans of a similar cruiser Carter had procured from a yacht sales organization, and now they knew their way about; they moved aft and into the cockpit, which was covered by an awning, and forward to the deckhouse. Down two steps was a closed door leading to the cabins. Opening her purse, taking out the pistol with the silencer, Sid gently tried the knob; it was locked. They could hear snoring.

Bill had his hand in his purse. His teeth glinted in an

overhead ray of light, and he whispered: "I'm glad I used my five-day deodorant—I'm perspiring."

She glanced at him doubtfully. "But the excitement's nice, isn't it?"

"Lovely, luv!"

Reassured, she pulled her scarf tighter around her face and knocked on the door. The snoring stopped. Grover T. Gaston stirred and mumbled inside. She repeated the knocking.

"Uh. Huh? Who is it, for Christ's sake?"

Sidney Ellen assumed her seductive voice, with which she had made a bit of money in the old days doing radio commercials. "It's me, Grover. Can I come in?"

"What? Who?"

"Grover! Little me! Let me in. I'm lonesome and dying for a drink."

"Uh. In a minute . . ."

Grunting, floundering, Grover arose. A light went on. The door lock clicked. He appeared—skinny, silver-haired, an unlovely sight in wrinkled pajamas. His yawn congealed, wide open, at the prodding of the automatic's muzzle.

"One word and I'll blow you apart. Turn around."

Grover turned. Sid moved aside to give Bill room. Grover was saying "Uh" when the sap hit the base of his skull in the area prescribed by Dr. Tilden. The sound was that of a melon being smartly slapped. He sank to his knees, and slid forward on his face.

Bill and Sid walked inside the combination galley and dining saloon, and Sid closed the door. She knelt at Grover's side, rolled him over, and made ready to apply the ether. Lighting a burner on the stove, Bill began warming the block of wax he carried, and went forward. When he returned, he had a watch and chain in his hand.

"All his stuff was in a drawer by his bunk," he said. "Here's the key—it's stamped 'Frontier Bank,' and it's got to be for a safe-deposit box. Number one-eleven.

The master's cabin is furnished in bad Victorian, with antimacassars and a little electric organ. Atrocious! But he's got some good Waterford glass."

"He's still breathing."

"What a pity."

Bill snapped the chain with a small pair of pliers, made an impression of the key, and tossed the end of the chain with key and fob on the floor beside Grover, who stirred and groaned and obligingly sucked in the ether Sid administered.

"It's hard doing anything in gloves," Bill said, cooling the wax under a faucet.

"Clean him out. Everything goes over the side."

"Everything? This is a good watch."

"Everything."

Roving through the boat, Bill gathered portable valuables. He loaded things in an empty suitcase weighted with a steam iron and tools, opened the door, crept to the stern, surveyed the marina, and dropped his load into the water. He made another trip with a second heavy piece of luggage.

"All that Waterford," he said. "And he has a few nice pieces of Georgian silver. His personal jewelry is terrible. . . . We can keep his cash, can't we? It's a good-sized roll."

"Yes. But tear everything apart, as though you were looking for more."

"Wait," Bill called, a little later. "He's got a coin collection. Hidden under his mattress, of all things. It looks valuable."

"Dump it."

"They're gold!"

"You heard me."

When he finished, Bill was breathing hard. He had worked fast. Sid gave Grover another application of the anesthetic and discarded the bottle and cotton. They left, closing and locking the door. Crouched in the deckhouse, they studied the scene. Nothing was stirring.

Sid deliberately enforced a slow pace back to the gate. As they approached it, a man appeared, came through, and strode in their direction. They recognized the watchman by his cap and the long flashlight he had. Sid's hand dipped into her purse.

"If necessary," she said softly, "we use the same technique as before. I stick him up and you belt him. Get it?"

"Yes, luv."

The watchman halted on the narrow walk in front of them, and they stopped and Sid said affably. "Good evening."

Peering at her shrouded face, the watchman said, "Good evening girls. Where're you from? I don't seem to remember you."

"Oh, we've been having a drink with Mr. Gaston on the *Bounty*," Sid said.

"Just having a few laughs," Bill added, in an authentic contralto.

The watchman grinned. "Yeah. Nice night for it, huh? Watch your step going out."

"Thank you very much," Sid said, with the dignity of a floozy, a role she had essayed several times in the movies.

As Bill passed the watchman, he flounced slightly. When they went through the gate, he and Sid had an opportunity to look back. The watchman was plodding on, and not even going in the direction of the deep-water moorings. They piled into the sedan, and Bill drove. Five miles off, he stopped at a telephone booth at a service station and Sid called Dr. Tilden, saying merely, "Okay. No strain. Meet us."

In Long Beach, two blocks from where she had parked her Buick, Brenda met them in the Cadillac with Biff; he took over the rental car and drove off, followed by Brenda. Sid and Bill walked to the parking lot. En route, two sportive sailors under the influence of drink whistled at them.

On the way back to Snug Harbor, along a residential street without traffic, Bill climbed over the front seat, huddled on the floor, divested himself of most of his feminine attire and his padding and his wig, scrubbed his face, put on slacks, turtleneck sweater and loafers ready to hand, and resumed his place beside Sid.

Carter and Sam were waiting for them at the front door. "Bless you," Carter said.

"It's so easy," Sid said. "I wonder why more people don't get into it?"

"Next comes the hard part," Sam said.

Grover wasn't found until late the next day. Actually, he wasn't found at all, and had to crawl out of the cabin of the *Bounty II* and down a walkway yelling hoarsely. He was suffering from a concussion and spent a couple of days in a hospital, in the grip of moderate trauma, and after he was released dared not return to his boat.

His misadventure got some mention in the Long Beach paper, but only a paragraph in the metropolitan press and a few words on radio and television. It was a familiar story, and Grover's habit of entertaining ladies of the evening led to obvious conclusions. His claim that he had suffered a loss to the thieves in excess of twenty thousand dollars was discounted liberally, in particular by the insurance company which held his floater policy—a fact which Biff went to some pains to ascertain. The watchman verified the presence of two women who had visited him that night, but said he could not hope to ever identify them, especially the one wearing the scarf, and was positive they were carrying nothing when he saw them leave the marina. Grover's denial that he had ever seen them before in his life and hadn't the least idea of who they were, and wouldn't know them again if he saw them, was received with incredulity; a man living that kind of life, and at his age, had to cover up.

Nobody got a license number. The stolen articles were never seen again. Investigating officers hazarded the opinion that the two women had male accomplices who had followed them and carried off the loot before the watchmen encountered them at the gate. Probably the men had been hidden in the back of the women's car. They said it was a thoroughly professional job, and that they thought they knew who the members of the gang were. Rounding them up was only a matter of time.

Grover came to the Snug Harbor country club wearing a plaster on the back of his head and an apprehensive look, and complained of headaches. His game was off and he lost wagers, thereby winning a little popularity. But members appreciatively quoted his ex-wife's remark when she heard of the incident. "I wish," she said, "that they'd caved in his skull. Even as it is, I'd send them a thank-you note if I knew where they were."

Carter supervised the allotting of Grover's cash on hand, which came to a surprising four hundred thirty-two dollars and sixty-one cents. In a graceful gesture, Bill bought a piece of Waterford with his share and put it in a place of honor in his trailer.

"It's the least I could do," he said. "I call it my concussion jar. I just don't know my own strength."

"I wonder if Grover will give up women," Sid said. She was alluding to the news that he had not pinched anyone in the club since the robbery. "I suppose not, really."

꙲꙲꙲꙲꙲꙲꙲ THEY STARTED calling themselves "the Seniles" because an erudite syndicated columnist, deploring the wave of student and minority revolt, as well as crime in the streets, revived the memory of the jewel robbery in Palm Springs. "Where will these profound tremors lead us?" he asked. "To the great amoral earthquake which will shake our ethical seismograph to pieces? What are these deep interpersonal interactions that threaten to destroy us, to write a coda for our civilization? Our former civility is vestigial, overlaid with profanation. 'Grandma bandits' are cognate with the nihilism of youth, and the last step comes when senility is no longer any bar to antisocial achievement." He called on President Nixon to forget antiballistic missiles and concentrate upon the malignancies at home.

The tribute bucked them up, especially Sidney Ellen, although she had to look up a number of words in the dictionary when she read the column. It had something to do with their deciding to take on the second phase of the job. But the main determinant arose from a disobeyal of orders by Bill Canary, to which he shamefacedly confessed after a time; on the night he ransacked *Bounty II,* he had been unable to resist stuffing in his purse a small, exquisite French cloisonné box found in Grover's chest of drawers. Later he discovered the box contained, besides sets of cufflinks and pearl and diamond stickpins and studs, several pairs of keys apparently intended for automobiles. Experimenting, he learned some of the keys would unlock the doors and ignition of his car; he surreptitiously tried them on Sid's new Buick and got the same result. When he came clean, Biff readily identified them.

"Master keys," he said. "Every auto dealer, finance company and thief has them. That's how the buggers get your car back when you fall behind in the payments. You've got a nice collection there."

Carter instantly conceived, full blown and splendid, an idea that solved many of the problems he and Sam were brooding upon. Involved were the informational services offered, prevailingly at no cost to themselves, by sanctimonious corporations. A public relations man in the power company in Long Beach had given Sam, who described himself on the telephone in a quavery voice as a concerned grandparent trying to help in a little boy's homework, exhaustive details of the south coast electrical grid system and various substations; Sam drew a rough sketch of the whole thing. And in pursuance of better community spirit the Frontier National Bank allowed a parochial school, which lacked space, to leave its buses nighttimes and weekends in the Yachtsmen's branch parking area. It all tied up in a neat package.

However, Carter, having appropriated the keys, first bawled out Bill, complimented him, and then told him to go and sin no more. He was forced to reduce the cloisonné box to rubble and destroy the jewelry. Despite Biff's assurance that they had in their possession free entry to a wide selection of trucks, semi-trailers, vans, pickups and campers, Sid was dispatched at night for a stroll around the Yachtsmen's branch to learn the make and model of the school buses. Thereafter, equipped by Bill with a moustache, toupee and glasses, Biff flew to San Francisco, had cards printed that identified him as manager of the Acme Collection Agency, and visited automobile dealers on Van Ness Avenue, who, harassed by deadbeats, were glad to be of assistance. He returned after two days and reported Bill had given them a pocketful of open sesames.

"Okay," Carter said. "We open the branch."

"Thanks to the fact that I love beautiful things," Bill said aggrievedly.

"Right," Biff said. "But what's a nice girl like you doing in a place like this?"

Nobody was amused. Decision had made the Seniles grim.

Timing was essential. Without exact coordination the effort would fail. Again and again, supervised by Sam and Carter, who prepared schedules and maps, they rehearsed their tasks and movements and made dry runs. Refusing to be hurried, Carter insisted on the study of every possible contingency; he was dead set against another Palm Springs foul-up.

Since this was going to require their full manpower, personnel difficulties plagued them. When Brenda learned she would have to steal a car and handle firearms, she paled and dissolved into tears. Only the news that she was going to wear the shortest of miniskirts, panty hose, a tight blouse, a fringed leather coat and a long fall partially revived her. But she was in good shape compared to Biff, also ashen and on the brink of crying as he heard he was to assist in cracking the bank.

"Uh, well . . ." he said; words stuck in his throat. "Say, wait. I—I see myself as more valuable doing the planning and furnishing the intelligence—I don't see myself going out and—"

"We do, Biff," Sam told him coldly. "We need a strong back. Were you under the impression you would always be able to play it safe while the rest of us did the dirty work?"

"Uh, no. But—"

"Everybody else has been out on the line. It's your turn now."

"We'd hate to have you refuse," Sidney Ellen said. "That might be awkward."

"Yeah," Biff said, scarcely above a whisper. "Yeah, I guess it would . . ."

Carter chafed under the nearly passive role he must assume. He yearned for action, but the discipline he had to enforce restricted his complaints. And he hated his job of driving the Cadillac.

"The damned glass is tinted," he said. "I can't see anything after dark."

Not very happy either, Bill looked his displeasure and said little. He had coveted and enjoyed the assignment of dressing up and going to the marina, but the glow of sapping Grover had dissipated, and he didn't like the new costume he would wear on the drudgery of having to go to the desert east of San Diego with Brenda and Sam and learn how to operate the machine pistol. Guns were not really his dish, and he and Brenda returned from successive daylong practice sessions in high, jumpy state.

"I'm going to run away before it happens," Brenda threatened. "Nobody could stand this. You wait and see. I hope Bill goes with me."

"Oh, no, dear," Bill said, and regarded her glumly. "Not that. Anything's better than that."

"Why, you little snip."

"Shall we start pulling each other's hair?"

"Dear God!" Carter said.

Equipment was considerable—weapons, flashlights, the kind of thick padding used for furniture by moving men, pinch bars, a sledgehammer, wire cutters, a high-intensity blowtorch, and glass-cutting tools. And a 20 mm. Hispano-Suiza aircraft machine cannon which Sam had bought several years before from a mail order arms house in Chicago, together with one hundred rounds of high explosive, instantaneous-impact-fused ammunition. During the preliminary period he had welded a lightweight tripod on which to mount the cannon, and fabricated a shield for the muzzle to hide the flash. During the trips to the desert with Bill and Brenda, he ignited samples of the shells with pistol fire to assure himself they remained live. In addition, Sid delivered two temporary California paper license strips, one removed from a new car, the other garnered from a trash can.

Biff was sent to Los Angeles to buy three walkie-talkies capable of transmitting and receiving at a distance of five to ten miles under optimum conditions.

Everything except the cannon was tested, including clothing to be worn. Brenda paraded for them in her outfit. She was enchanted by what she saw in the mirror and forgot less pleasant aspects; her bust was high and protruding, her calves and thighs fully revealed in a mere suggestion of a skirt, her dark wig a disorderly, concealing veil that fell below her shoulders. Heavy makeup wiped out years. To complement her, Bill wore skin-tight yellow pants, a silk blouse opened on his chest, a moldy old hussar's jacket, boots and a yachting cap. He was heavily bearded, profusely haired, and had on antique steel-rimmed spectacles.

"I must say," Brenda said, "that for a woman almost forty I don't look it."

"Of course you don't, luv," Bill said. "But that's because you're almost fifty, isn't it?"

"You look like General Grant!"

Bill shrugged sadly. "General Lee, darling, I'm a loser."

To avoid any suggestion of the "Grandma Bandit" image, Sid wore a dark wig, no powder and paint, a simple skirt and shirtwaist, and glasses. Biff and Sam put on coveralls that had ST. MARK'S SCHOOL printed on them, and khaki caps with long bills like those worn by naval officers on active duty. Alone among them, Car-

Come discover the Kotex Kotique

Find yourself a "for real" feminine deodorant

Kotique feminine deodorant spray. Not just another perfumey cover-up. But a unique formula from Kotex that deals with the *cause* of the matter.

Truly effective—but ever so gentle.

Just one of the many new feminine freedoms you will find in the Kotique Collection by Kotex.

For a 3 oz. size of Kotique feminine deodorant spray, send your name, address and 50¢ to: Kotique, Box 551, Neenah, Wis. 54956. Indicate mist or powder. Offer expires June 30, 1972.

LANCERS. FOR THE GOOD LIFE.

The imported rosé from Portugal, in the crock as distinctive as the wine it contains.

ter was attired in an ordinary suit, shirt and tie; but he had the moustache Biff had worn to San Francisco, and bushy gray eyebrows.

There was more to it than that. Each of them had alternate clothing, worn underneath if possible, or at least susceptible to quick change, and a face mask. These other garments were also costumes—Brenda was a ballet dancer in a tutu, Bill a thinly clad distance runner with a number on his back, Sid a gypsy, Biff a pirate, Carter a clown, Sam an Arab in flowing robe and burnous. The costumes lent practice sessions a surrealistic atmosphere that bemused them (and infatuated Brenda). Their dress was dictated by Carter's choice for the job of a Saturday night which happened to be the occasion of the annual Golden Years masked costume ball given at the main assembly hall. Admission was ten dollars per person, refreshments were free, dancing went on until dawn, customarily several revelers overdid and departed feet first in ambulances. Proceeds above expenses were devoted to the improvement of library and recreational facilities. The Seniles would attend the ball—in due course.

Although this particular evening added to the complications of preparing for the raid, Carter was quick to defend his decision. Saturday nights were busy ones for the cops, especially in summer; they always had their hands full then and would be more widely spread. Assuming disguises was manifestly easier under such conditions. The general confusion in Golden Years would help to cover movements of the gang. And—God forbid—if something went wrong and they needed to disappear, what better place could they find than the masked mob in the assembly hall?

Inevitably, with all other details smoothed out, the question of the feasibility and power of the old Hispano-Suiza aircraft cannon arose. No possible means of testing it was available, and success hinged on its performance. They had to rely on Sam's calculations and

assurances. He shook his head stubbornly at the suggestion he include safecracking explosives in his arsenal.

"They're hard to buy and unpredictable," he said.
"That's how the cops would track us down. And that's
how you get hurt, handling the stuff. I don't agree. You
could get your head knocked off."

"Yes, you could!" Biff said, in a new alto voice. "I
don't agree either...."

Sam did consent to taking along a high-speed electric
drill that would run off an auto battery, and diamond
drills which Biff could pound into the masonry with the
sledgehammer in an emergency.

"I wonder what Mr. Gaston will do," Brenda said, at
their last run-through.

"We haven't got his money yet," Sid replied.

"I mean if he comes to the ball, and sees me in my
tutu."

Sid looked despairingly around. Her eyes stopped on
Biff. He was staring at Brenda in her tutu.

The afternoon was warm, humid and smoggy. During the course of it, driving with the slow caution of the
fabled old lady from Pasadena, Carter took Brenda to
that city and allowed her to circulate in a number of
department store parking lots. She was dressed in ordinary, inconspicuous matron's clothing, her face pretty
much hidden by a floppy Milan straw hat and big dark
glasses.

Brenda was edgy and querulous. She repeatedly said,
in divers forms: "And I thought when I married a doctor a lot older than me I at least was getting security.
Some security! Now I have to steal cars!"

He didn't argue with her, and only reiterated his
stern orders at intervals. Once she wept; he paid no attention. While she inspected unoccupied cars, he stood
guard. Carter was selective, counting on the ingrained
habit Southern Californians had for buying new auto-

mobiles and hoping to find one still awaiting license plates. He waved Brenda away from several good prospects.

The fifth location they covered yielded what he wanted—a pristine sports car bearing a temporary sticker on the rear bumper. Obedient to his imperative gesture after he had made sure they were unobserved, Brenda, shaking visibly, got into the Corvette and drove off. Carter followed her, and a few miles away they stopped on a little-traveled street beside a vacant lot. Using rubber cement, he quickly pasted his own temporary license over the existing one, and deliberately paused to draw breath. His wife, aside from glancing jerkily over her shoulder every few seconds, was gaining in cheer.

"Carty, you won't believe this," she said. "I didn't have to use the master keys. Some idiot left his keys in the ignition. How careless can you get?"

"Never mind," he said. "I'll meet you in Long Beach a block south of the parking lot."

Brenda far surpassed his plodding pace, put the Corvette in a crowded downtown lot, and awaited him on the corner. She was positively gay now.

"Boy, that 'Vette is a bomb," she said. Because her most enduring interest, except for clothes and the preservation of youth, was in cars, she read the motor magazines each month and had a fund of inside lingo. "It's got four on the floor, discs all around, plenty of cubes up front for vaa-rooom, and racing skins. You ought to see how it handles, Carty!"

He gazed at her in astonishment and mild annoyance. "Really? Perhaps I'll buy you one someday."

"Would you, darling? That'd be wonderful!"

They gathered after sundown at the Tilden house, tense and a trifle sweaty; the coming of night had not lowered the temperature much. Their last briefing was protracted. No drinking was permitted despite Biff's whining plea for a single straight shot. They had coffee and sandwiches, and Carter distributed pills.

"Just a little Perphenazine and Amitriptyline," he said. "You'll brighten up and be relieved of your anxieties. They're good for the elderly."

Everyone did brighten up.

But time dragged. Finally Carter ordered them to synchronize their watches. Sam and Biff went into the garage, where Sam's car was parked beside the Cadillac, and transferred equipment; when they were ready to go back inside they raised the door. The walkie-talkies were tested and stowed. Weapons and ammunition were handed out—Sid had her familiar automatic, Brenda the machine pistol, Bill the Luger, Carter a compact little Walther he could hide in the palm of his hand, and Sam a .45 caliber service issue giant he had carried in his Army days. Then put on disguises and outfits; the bulky spares went into paper sacks. Masks were donned. Sid felt in her purse for the master keys she had received from Brenda.

"A final reminder," Carter said. "This will succeed only through perfect timing and close communication. We have to keep in touch constantly. If there is any breakdown in that, we call it off. But once Sam signals he is in the vault, the job goes on regardless. If you can't make a rendezvous point, or something really bad goes wrong, you'll be informed; then you simply scatter and get back to the ball as best you can. Remember your codes—somebody is bound to be listening in on our transmissions. . . . All right. Let's go."

Bill gave a stiff, spread-eagled British salute. "Okay, chaps," he said. "We're for it."

They marched outside, laughing and talking according to Carter's instructions; after he had backed out the Cadillac, Biff lowered the garage door and they climbed in. A sedan passed, and the masked, costumed people in it waved and shouted. Sid blew them a kiss and Carter sounded his horn.

All of Golden Years was full of cars and pedestrians in weird garb and extremely alive. At the main assembly hall was a traffic jam. However, many of the cars were departing because "refreshments" at the ball always consisted of weak punch and unfilling finger sandwiches, and experienced celebrants liked to escape briefly and stoke up on cocktails and food; the Golden Glow Inn and Happy Talk Cafeteria were full to overflowing on these nights. The Seniles merged unnoticed in the outgoing stream.

They removed their masks and everyone but Carter scrunched down in his seat. He stopped beyond reach of streetlights beside a warehouse to allow Sam to remove the license plates and Bill to gum the temporary license strip on the rear window. Then Carter exceeded his usual pokey speed. In Long Beach, without a word being exchanged, he halted past the parking lot and walked back to retrieve the Corvette; it had been deemed unwise for Brenda to be seen in her mod attire, which might stick in an attendant's memory.

Getting into the low-slung car was painful to the doctor. He knocked off his hat. The stiff clutch and the gearshift were a trial to him. A young man at the entrance who took his ticket and payment grinned at him.

"That's a wild beast you got there, sir," he remarked.

"Much too wild," Carter said. "It's my daughter's. She went to the beach with her boyfriend and couldn't come to pick it up."

He let out the clutch too quickly, made the rear tires squawk, and killed the engine. The young man laughed condescendingly. Carter had difficulty restarting the car, killed it again, and had to accept advice from the young man. As he drove away, he was silently cursing himself for attracting attention and offering gratuitous information; it was going badly right at the beginning, and he was at fault for not having schooled himself beforehand in driving the Corvette.

Stopping behind his own car, he pried himself out and waited while Brenda quickly took his place at the wheel. Bill sat beside her and began to unwrap the package that contained his walkie-talkie.

"Carty, I'm scared," she said. "I hate guns."

"So am I," Carter said, "and sometimes I hate you."

He limped forward to the Cadillac, almost disposed to ask Sam to drive during the first phase; but putting off his hour of trial was useless. His participation as a motorist in this was essential and crucial even though he had only a limited one-year driving license. A foreboding impulse to cancel the operation crossed his mind. He put it down, hooked his glasses over his ears, and stared grumpily ahead through the tinted windshield. Sam was unlimbering his and Carter's walkie-talkies.

The first transmissions started. Reception was not very good—raspy and crackling. Some messages had to be repeated. Sam's code name was Able, Bill was Baker, Carter would be Charley.

"Halfway," Bill reported. "No sweat. Baker out."

"Roger," Sam replied. He checked his watch under the map light and made a whirling motion with a forefinger to Carter, urging him to speed up. "Charley running slow. Baker orbit. Acknowledge. Over."

"Roger, Baker. Out."

Presently Bill called: "Charley advise. Long time. Over."

Carter was going faster, hunched over the wheel, peering forward in a rapture of concentration that had caused his jaw to drop. Crouched in the rear, Sidney Ellen and Biff bumped heads when the car rounded a corner.

"I feel like going to the bathroom," Biff whispered. His eyes seemed enormous to her in a flash from a streetlamp, his pallor quite apparent. She was disgusted, and aware of panicky fear.

Sam looked around him, glanced at his sketch map and watch, and held the walkie-talkie mike to his lips. "Four minutes. Go in, Baker. Stand by. Acknowledge. Over."

"Roger, Charley. Out."

A couple of cars passed them, exhibited beaming ruby taillights, and vanished. They went through the deserted little business section. The air had salt in it, the smell of tidal waters. Ahead glowed the short, squat amber column of the Yachtsmen's branch. Carter slowed abruptly and cut off his headlights; he crept foot by foot into the bank parking section and stopped in the lee of three smallish yellow school buses. He left his engine running, but it was so quiet at idle that it made almost no sound.

Jumping out of the car, Sam stood listening and looking, his breath held. He could detect neither movement nor noise within his compass. Leaning into the front seat, bent over the walkie-talkie, he said: "Baker. Baker. Over."

"Baker standing by. Over."

"No sweat. Strike. Over."

"Roger, Charley. Striking minus three. Out."

Sid and Biff plunged from the Cadillac, the former with the Able walkie-talkie. Sam, who had the second set of keys to the car, went to the rear and unlocked the trunk. He and Biff grunted under the weight of the machine cannon, which weighed well over a hundred pounds. Scrambling, Sid helped with the smaller items. Running, stumbling, staggering, they brought the cannon to the building. They raced back and forth, piling everything beside it. Sid thought how ironical Sam's "no sweat" message had become—they were all sweating heavily now.

Sam spoke to her gaspingly; she was forgetting her duty as guard. She stopped the fetching, took out her gun, pulled back the action to put a shell in the chamber, and went to lurk in the shadow of one of the buses.

An instant afterward every light on that part of the coast went off.

A mile and an eighth away, not far from the sea, set off a short distance from a few small industrial buildings and a block from the nearest houses, was a substantial gravelly plot surrounded by six-foot-high chainlink fence topped with three strands of barbed wire; inside the enclosure, fed by heavy voltage cables, was the substation.

Brenda swung up to it without lights and left the engine on. She and Bill jumped out, steadying their guns on the low roof of the car.

"Stop sobbing, luv," Bill said, not unkindly.

He was the first to open fire on the assemblage of transformers and ceramic insulators, and then Brenda got off a burst. When his gun was empty, he snatched the machine pistol from her, put in a fresh magazine, and fired two more bursts. Lightning flashed and hissed, metal shrieked, insulators rang bell-like and dissolved. They were caught up in an ecstasy of destruction and were no longer frightened.

Darkness engulfed them. Something caught fire in the substation and cast an intense, brief light.

"Let's go!" Bill said.

They literally bounced into the Corvette. Brenda took off with howling tires before Bill could close the door on his side. Even as he did, he heard the sound of startled cries and a minor explosion behind the fence which produced another brief glare. The car seemed to crouch and claw, at the earth when Brenda shifted smoothly into second and then third. She put on the headlights coming up to an intersection, and at the same moment other headlights glared at them from the cross street—a black-and-white car was almost in their path.

"Oh, mercy . . ." Bill breathed, and instinctively grabbed for the machine pistol.

Braking powerfully, Brenda swung left, on the thin edge of going out of control, and the cops—Bill could see two of them, for the cars were within a foot of collision—turned right and slid to a stop.

"Hang on," Brenda said. "I'm going to stand on it."

Bill's seat threatened to slide from under him, and the engine screamed. His eyes were riveted on Brenda. He was frozen. He could not swallow. But Brenda was half smiling. Her hands gripped the wheel in the approved eleven and two o'clock position; she was using gears to aid the brakes; she drifted through a curve scarcely losing revs. Behind them red lights blinked on and a siren ululated.

Bill repressed a desire to close his eyes; he remembered his training. He picked up the walkie-talkie and said, with commendable calm: "Baker calling. Fuzz. That's all. Out."

Bill's transmission came to the Able group as an awful shock. According to plan, Carter had crept away in the darkened Cadillac when the lights went out. Sam was slicing part of a pane from the darkened Yachtsmen's branch—the glass was thick and tough and hard to cut, and he had to exert his whole strength. By his side stood Biff, ready to help, holding a flashlight with a dimmed lens on the work. At their feet was the walkie-talkie, reception turned low.

"Oh, Jesus . . ." Biff said; the faded beam he was pointing at the window wavered.

Unable to hear what had been received, Sid hastened across to them. Sam whispered, "Baker must have run into cops on the way out. Just hard luck—"

Carter had heard Bill. "Able. Charley. Shall we cancel? Over."

Sam stood stiffly for thirty seconds, breathing hard; his companions watched him cataleptically. Then he dropped to his knees, and Biff lowered his light to hold the walkie-talkie. Sam's mean face looked meaner than ever.

"Charley," he said. "Able. Proceeding. Orbit. Acknowledge. Over."

"Able. Charley. Disapprove. But orbiting. Out."

"You can count on Carter," Sam said. "At least Baker will draw off the cops, and if they keep their mouths shut if they get caught. . . . Anyway, we're in too deep. Come on!"

Returning to her post, Sid glared desperately into the darkness; she could see nothing. It was difficult for her to hear because of the blood pounding in her ears, but she thought she detected a distant sound of mingled voices and police sirens.

The struggle with the glass went on, and Sam produced new tools. Finally he cursed and thumped on the section he had weakened with a gloved, clenched hand. Neither he nor Biff could prevent its sudden collapse and shattering fall inward. The noise seemed tremendous; they waited rigidly for a little while, wondering at the silence that still obtained.

Sid heard the glass breaking and flinched. She was engaged in opening the door of one of the buses, something she had been briefed to do as soon as they arrived at the bank; she reproved herself cruelly for getting rattled and forgetting. Now she ignored the men struggling to get the cannon, tripod, ammunition belts, mats and tools into the building, and concentrated on her task. In a moment she was inside the bus, found the correct key for the ignition switch and turned it on, and checked the gasoline gauge. Next she choked and started the engine, immediately shutting it off. She slid off the seat to the running board and thence to the ground, left the door open, and picked up the pistol she had laid aside. The night remained implacably hooded and silent.

[98]

There were two loud thumps. "What's that?" Brenda shouted above the roar of the motor.

"I saw flashes," Bill said. "I think they're shooting at us—maybe with a shotgun. But they are losing ground."

"No lousy squad car could catch *this*."

"Others could. They must be calling on their radio."

"Brace yourself."

An alley was coming up. Bill decided she could not possibly make the turn, closed his eyes, and grabbed the padded dash. The motor howled in a downshift, brakes dragged sickeningly, tires shrieked in agony. A fender splintered a board fence and crumpled. They went down the alley in second gear, the tachometer needle touching the red line. Bill's eyes were open again—he was unable to bear not seeing his end. Nobody, he thought, would now be sleeping in these houses. He looked back, heard the siren and screeching brakes and tires, and saw the red-lighted black-and-white go sailing by.

"They missed," he said, "but maybe they'll have the sense to circle the block."

"So what," Brenda replied calmly. "They've lost the race."

She turned right at the alley exit, backtracking, and left at the first corner. A car was approaching in the opposite direction, and Brenda, cutting across, fanned it with perhaps five inches to spare; the car lurched toward the curb and stopped, and the Corvette went by so fast that Bill's vision blurred. Two blocks farther on she turned right again, and left a couple of times more. She slowed down. They had outrun the sound of the police siren.

"I bet that guy who was coming up to the corner will never be the same again," she said.

"Neither will I."

"Doesn't it look funny without a light on anywhere?"

It was eerie, and they felt pleasure in contemplating

the results of their handiwork. The headlights of passing automobiles looked extraordinarily bright. Candles and flashlights illuminated a few houses. A brooding silence had fallen.

"We've got to get rid of this car," Brenda said. "I can hear the left front tire hitting on the busted fender."

"Find an apartment house and go in back," Bill said. "That's our emergency instruction."

They spotted an imposing modern building with balconies and picture windows and sliding glass doors, and Brenda swung into the driveway and drove to the rear where the carports were, stopping in an empty stall between two sedans. She cut off the engine and lights. The apartment house was quiet and dark except for a single feeble glow in a second-story room.

"How about the Pontiac?" Brenda whispered.

"Okay."

When they were out of the Corvette and had gathered their possessions, they softly closed the doors. The duplicate set of master car keys Sam had made were in Bill's hand—his other hand held the machine pistol— and he unlocked the Pontiac. Brenda took the wheel, started the engine and put on the lights, and backed out. They went down the driveway unhindered and motored sedately away.

"Get rid of that fall," Bill ordered. "Wipe off the makeup."

He removed his beard and excess hair, and squirmed out of the hussar's jacket and silk blouse, sitting revealed in the runner's costume; the boots, spectacles and yachting cap were tossed into the rear, and he put on tennis shoes. Then he held the wheel while Brenda struggled to rid herself of outer clothing and pull up her tutu.

"You mustn't look," she said.

"Oh, I won't, darling," he said. "I wouldn't peek if we were in a Turkish bath together."

As they passed a small park, he asked her to stop,

gathered their discarded garments, got out, dropped the clothing in a trash can, replaced the lid, and returned. Brenda drove on. A few minutes later they encountered two police cars, running without red lights or sirens. In both vehicles the cops on the right side were riding shotgun.

Dangling an arm back over the seat to make sure the guns and walkie-talkie were hidden by a lap robe he had found in the Pontiac, Bill said, "Remember we're going to the Golden Years ball if they stop us. Have you got the fake address in your head?"

"Yes. And I'm your girl friend."

"Just for a minute, luv."

But the police gave them only a cursory inspection in passing, one putting the beam of a powerful flashlight on the Pontiac.

"Exciting, isn't it, dear?"

"I'm beginning to have an empty feeling," Brenda said.

When they were in the clear, Bill got the walkie-talkie and fiddled with it. "Baker. No sweat now. Will orbit rendezvous. Acknowledge and give status. Over."

Carter answered promptly: "Charley. Proceed. Orbiting. Status: in progress. Out."

Nothing was heard from Able.

Able did not hear either message because Sam had the cannon assembled and covered by mats (Biff held another to the opening in the glass) and was firing at the vault from a distance of fifteen feet. The noise of the muzzle blasts and the shells hitting concrete and metal was thunderous despite the cotton in their ears. Debris flew through and fogged the air. A stink of burnt powder arose.

The Hispano-Suiza toppled over, felling Sam under the mats. He swore. The quiet that followed was nearly as alarming as the clamor.

"I didn't build the tripod heavy enough," he said, crawling out. "Get Sid."

Biff went for her. "Sam wants you. See anything?"

"No."

"How did it sound outside?"

"Not very loud."

Sam told her to put cotton in her ears. Somehow he had wrestled the cannon upright and was realigning it.

"It's the goddam recoil," he said. "All these blowback pieces are unsteady. The two of you get down there and hold the mount."

"That close?" Biff quavered. "I think we ought to go, Major."

Sam's fury was undiluted. "Another word and I'll put you in front of the piece, you son of a bitch!"

On her knees, braced against Biff, under the mats, Sidney Ellen was bathed in sweat. Her eyes filmed; she was weeping in her excitement and agitation. When the cannon ripped out a burst, paused, and resumed firing, she clung desperately to the tripod and wondered how soon her brains would be reduced to jelly; of course she would never hear again. Hot empty shells cascaded on her. Then the covering was torn away, and she staggered to her feet with ringing head. In the thin radiance of the work light on the floor Biff's wet face shone like a colorless moon. Sam looked maniacal.

"The goddam thing is fouling because it's air cooled," he said. "We won't use the padding if I can get it going again."

He seized tools and a cartridge extractor, snapping an order for Biff to bring the light closer. His heavy gloves burned and stank where they came into contact with the fiery breech and heat dissipation baffles on the barrel. Sid wheeled, wobbling, and turned her pencil flashlight on the vault wall. It was crumbling!

"All right," Sam said. "Grab hold. Here we go—I hope."

"But somebody'll hear us without the covering—" Biff started to say.

"No they won't," Sid said. She shoved Biff down. "The building's so soundproofed you can't hear much outside. Didn't I tell you?"

They hung on once more, and Sam inserted a steel shim to raise the elevation of the cannon. The clatter, smashing and successive explosions were excruciating. The bombardment appeared to last for an infinity. In the aching silence that followed, Sid and Biff rose groggily to their feet. Sam was speaking, but they couldn't hear him. He moved closer to them.

"Nearly a whole belt that time," he said pridefully. "The damn thing was firing at a rate of five hundred rounds a minute." Stooping, he swiveled the work light. "Look!"

A gaping hole marred the vault wall where it broke the circular sweep of the counter. The Yachtsmen's branch was littered with wreckage; chunks of steel-latticed masonry had flown outward and smashed everything in their trajectories. A miasma of smoke, dust and acrid fumes made them wheeze.

"Put it into the water, big boy," Sam said.

With his help, Biff got the cannon and tripod on his shoulders. As Sid steadied him, he groaned and said, "Now I *know* I'm going to wear a truss."

The walkie-talkie at their feet spoke quietly: "Able. Charley. Did you read? Can you read? Baker orbiting. Charley orbiting. You have exceeded maximum time. Beware lights coming on. Acknowledge. Over."

"Good," Sam said. "Baker got away." He picked up the radio. "Able. Shut up. Stand by. Out."

"I think we ought—" Biff began.

"You shut up too," Sam growled.

He took a sack and started gathering up the empty shell casings. Sid helped him. Lumbering to the aperture in the glass, Biff lowered the cannon, shoved it through, and followed it.

"Don't show too much light when you help him, Sid," Sam said, and handed her the sack. "Make him throw it in deep water. The minute you're through, stand guard again." He glanced regretfully over his shoulder. "I hate to lose that piece. . . ."

Sid went after Biff. He had his load hoisted once more, and she aided as best she could. Her pencil light, directed at the ground, was not of much assistance. When they left the asphalted section, he stumbled repeatedly. Once he fell, and although he pitched the cannon ahead of him, the barrel banged him on the head. He lay gasping feebly, and Sid had to shake him to get him to his knees. She strained with all her might to help in raising the cannon to his shoulders. At last they arrived at a concrete bulkhead which protected the point of land and Biff set the cannon on it and started to shove.

"No!" Sid hissed. "Throw it farther out. Sam's orders."

"Sid, I can't! I'm beat. I'm an old man—"

"You heard me." She prepared to draw her gun.

Biff groaned and climbed onto the bulkhead. Sid scrambled up behind him and helped to elevate the cannon; Biff heaved it mightily into the sea, and almost followed in its wake; she caught him by the slack of his coveralls and jerked him to her. They performed an absurd balancing act and fell on the landward side of the wall. Fortunately, he did not fall on her. It was a little while before they could arise.

"I'm done for," Biff said. "I'm going to retire. I mean really retire. I wish I'd never met any of you—"

"Oh, knock it off," Sid said.

She ascended the wall and hurled the sack as far as she could. Then she rejoined Biff and accompanied him to the bank. He crawled inside, and she went back to the bus.

Floundering in the dark after tripping on the mats, Biff knocked over the walkie-talkie. The faintest of glows came from the hole in the vault. He crept to it and saw Sam standing in front of the serried rows of gleaming metal doors of the larger safe-deposit boxes, one door open. Sam pulled out the box, put it on the floor, and raised the lid. His gloved fingers flickered clumsily in prying up the flaps of thick envelopes. Fresh, hopeful expectation invigorated Biff.

"It's me, Sam," he called softly. "What've you got?"

"The stuff is here, by Judas!" Sam said. "Mostly in thousand-dollar bills!"

"Box one-eleven . . ." Biff said. "That's a lucky number."

"There's a hell of a lot," Sam said. "Maybe a couple of hundred thousand."

He emptied the black box of everything, stuffed papers and envelopes into a sack, returned the box to its crypt, closed and locked the door, muttered to himself "Replace bank keys," and did so in a cabinet near the grilled steel door at the vault entrance, retrieved the light, and joined Biff. He picked up his tool kit and gestured to Biff to take the walkie-talkie.

"Leave the rest," he commanded. "Let's go!"

They dived through the hole in the glass and ran uncertainly to the buses, for Sam had doused his light. When she saw them, Sid entered the bus and started the engine. Biff and Sam sat down behind her.

"Don't turn on the headlights," Sam said. "Feel your way out of here. We're far behind schedule."

"Did you find anything?" she asked.

"Yes. Plenty. Listen, don't drive this the way you did that station wagon in Palm Springs."

She told herself to be calm. She had been thoroughly instructed on how to handle that model bus, but it was very unwieldy. Backing out inch by inch, she turned and rolled haltingly from the Yachtsmen's branch parking lot and into the business area.

"Lights," Sam said.

She turned them on and increased speed.

"Did you see anything?" he said.

"One car just before you came," she said. "It went away without stopping."

"I'll get in touch," Sam said. "I hope to God they haven't panicked."

He fiddled with the radio, spoke into it, waited. Nothing happened.

"The light doesn't come on," he said. "It's not working. What the hell has happened to the thing?"

A chill spread over Biff. "It was all right before," he said. "Are you pressing the right button?"

"Mind your own business." Sam sighed. "All right. It's kaput. Head for the alternate rendezvous, Sid. I'll tell you when to stop."

Sliding lower in the seat, squinting through the windshield, Carter endeavored to keep passing motorists from observing that he was using the short-wave transmitter. "Able. Able. Advise. Time running out, Advise. Urgent. Over."

Nothing. The set crackled.

"Able. This is Charley orbiting. Do you read me? Do you read me? Come in. Over."

Finally Baker came in: "Charley. Baker. Advise. Do we abort? Fuzz near. Over."

Carter drew a deep breath. He wasn't afraid, but the constant driving, especially with one hand, was a great chore. "Baker. Charley. Get off the air. We do not abort if it takes all night. Out."

Lights went on along the south coast. The sudden radiance was blinding.

"That does it," Sam said. "They've switched around and restored the power. The alarms will start going off in the bank, and pretty soon they'll notice the missing bus and look for it." A note of despair invaded his voice. "This goddam business has gone wrong from the start."

In a moment he got hold of himself. A small park attracted his attention.

"Okay," he said. "Abandon ship. Sid, drop us off. Go around the block and put the bus in an alley. See those lights in the center of the park? They're the public toilets. Meet us in the men's side."

He and Biff dropped off, clutching their belongings. There was no time to see if people were around; they simply ran into protecting shrubbery. Sid drove in stifling fear to the next intersection, waited for a single car to go by before making a left turn, and turned again at an alley. As she went down it, she switched off the lights. To her amazement, she found herself at the rear of a closed used car lot. Plenty of space was available. She drove in among the automobiles, stopped the bus, gathered what she had to carry, and ran back down the alley. At the street she slowed down, not from caution and decision but from sheer lung-bursting inability to do more. It took her several minutes to reach the park. Just after she crossed the street, a police car, siren and red lights on, roared toward the ocean.

The neighborhood was restive. Lights were on and she could hear people talking. But the park was deserted, and she made her way to the toilets and entered the men's side.

"It's me," she called before she went through the doorway. In spite of her exhaustion and knife-edged tension, she felt ill-at-ease and hesitant—she had never been in a men's toilet.

"Come on in," Biff said.

Already dressed in his pirate's costume, a handkerchief bound around his head, a patch over his left eye, he was holding Sam's .45 awkwardly; he handed it to Sam, who had finished dressing in robe and burnous and rubbing on dark makeup supplied by Bill.

"All right?" Sam said to Sid.

"As far as I know. I don't think I was seen. The bus is in the rear of a used car lot."

"Good. Get into your clothes. I'll try to repair the radio. If I can't, we'll have to find a phone and call a cab. Our story is that we're from Laguna and heading for the Golden Years ball and our car broke down after we got lost and the auto club towed it away. Got it?"

"Yes."

"Yeah," Biff said. His complexion was sadly faded.

Avoiding looking at a row of urinals, Sid went primly into a cubicle, stripped off her outer clothing, dispensed with the spectacles, and put on blouse, skirt, bandana and sash. She added a pair of dangling golden earrings.

When she came out, Sam was squatting on the floor, his tool packet open and the walkie-talkie partly disassembled.

"The aerial's been bent and the connection broken," he said. "I think I can fix it. Who the devil did this?"

Biff turned from them, and Sid stared at his back. But Sam was too busy to take note of that and continued working.

They heard men's voices and the sound of footsteps. Sam grabbed his automatic and jumped up.

"Get ready," he snapped. "Put on your masks."

Sid released the safety on her pistol. She stepped to one side of the door, Sam to the other, and Biff moved behind them. Two young sailors in uniform, both a bit high, walked in. The guns commanded their immediate attention. The appearance of the trio confronting them glazed their eyes.

"Put your arms behind you," Sam said.

"We've spent all our money," the man in the lead said.

"Is this a joke?" the second man said.

"It won't be if you keep talking," Sam replied. "Turn your backs to us." He motioned to Biff. "We're going to bind and gag you, and you won't get hurt if you cooperate."

Biff produced a pocketknife, cut strips out of discarded clothing, and used cord that had held together some of their impedimenta and the electrical line intended to run from the storage battery to the high-speed drill. One sailor struggled in his grasp, and he applied sudden pressure; the sailor cried, "Ouch!" and subsided.

The other sailor said plaintively, "I have to go to the bathroom. That's why we came in here."

"You can wait," Sid told him. "You're young."

"You're no lady, madam," the sailor said.

When their hands had been bound behind them and gags had been applied, Biff shoved them into cubicles in sitting positions, secured their ankles, and closed the doors. They made mooing sounds and he reproved them. Sam had already returned to tinkering with the radio. After a few moments he had it back together. He went to the doorway for better transmission, Sid in advance of him, gun ready. Biff gathered the rest of their stuff.

"Well, here goes," Sam said. "I'm going to have to give our position. If Baker and Charley have quit, we're on our own."

"I wouldn't blame them for quitting," Sid said.

"I would," Biff said. "To my dying day—which could be tonight."

Sam said: "Able. Able calling. Acknowledge. Over."

There was a gratifying rush to reply; both Baker and Charley were immediately on the air.

"Charley, Charley," Sam said. "Do you read? Over."

"Charley. I read you. Over."

"Position Padre Serra Park. North side, midway. Give time. Urgent. Over."

"Minus fifteen, Able. Confirm. Over."

"Roger, Charley. Out." Sam shook his head. "That's a long time, but it's so hard for the poor old guy to drive at night. . . ."

They heard Charley go on the air again: "Baker,

Pickup—minus about six. Rendezvous alternate three. Acknowledge. Over."

"Baker. Roger. Out."

The sailors were stirring in their pens. Going inside, Sid said, "Keep moving, kids, and you'll end up full of holes."

Their struggles ceased. She rejoined her companions. Sam was gone, and Biff was carrying their odds and ends, plus the walkie-talkie.

"I've aged ten years," Biff said.

"You should have," Sid retorted, "after busting that radio!"

"You're crazy!" he hissed.

As he glared at her, Sam came back from his scouting trip and said, "It looks all right. Follow me and do what I do." He took the radio from Biff. "When we come to a refuse can, dump everything in. Move out."

They followed him closely, in single file, from one clump of vegetation to another. Biff stopped at a can and unburdened himself.

Sam turned. "Take off your masks, you damned fools!" A moment later, he added: "Here comes somebody. Take cover."

Dropping, crawling, they found shelter amid flowering shrubs. A woman walking her fat, apathetic poodle crossed the lawn to their left; the dog paused indecisively, sniffing the air, felt the tug of his leash, and ambled on. Sam waited and then arose, lifting the burnous and rubbing his damp brow. He had the walkie-talkie secreted under his robe.

"Don't hurry," he said. "Take it easy . . ."

He led them to the edge of the park and found luxuriant shrubbery under which they could lie prone and feel their hearts laboring against earth wetted by dew. Waiting was frightful. Time halted. A police car went by. Biff breathed loudly through his nose.

Sam held out his wrist to catch the gleam of a street-lamp on his watch. "Running late," he whispered.

"Late. We'll give them five minutes. Then we'll dump the radio and take off. But don't ask me what the hell we'll do exactly . . ."

It seemed to Sidney Ellen that five hours elapsed. Sam was gathering his knees under him when he saw the Cadillac slowly coming down the street; he stood up wrenchingly and surveyed the situation.

"Okay," he said. "Move out. On the double."

Breaking from the greenery, they ran madly for the car. Brenda was at the wheel, Bill and Carter in the front seat beside her. She barely stopped as the Able contingent piled into the rear. Sid was thumped on the head by Biff's elbow (he was in the lead), and Sam received the heel of Sid's left slipper in his mouth—the blow puffed his lips and dislodged his partial upper plate.

"Get onto the highway," Carter said to Brenda. "Back to Golden Years. . . . My God, what a night!"

"Did you find anything?" Bill asked.

When he could talk, Sam said, "I've got a bag of money strapped to my waist. I don't know how much."

"No matter how much," Carter said, "it wouldn't be enough for what's happened to us tonight."

Now there came a pride of black-and-whites, but the Cadillac was not molested. The main coastal road was heavily congested. Something was holding up traffic beyond a mere Saturday night rush. Then they observed blinking red and yellow lights ahead.

"It's a roadblock!" Carter said.

"Oh, Jesus," Biff said. "They're shaking down everybody. You should have counted on that."

Brenda was in the curbside lane. She crept toward the next corner, preparing to turn.

"No," Carter decided. "Keep in line. We'd only attract attention."

"I could outrun them," Brenda said.

"You're Juan Fangio," Bill said, "but even you wouldn't have a chance."

As Brenda smiled, Sam said, "Hide the goddam radios."

They were put underfoot.

"Listen to me," Carter said. "We're all from down the coast, on the way to meet friends at the ball—"

"Laguna," Sam said.

"Yes, Laguna. If they find the walkie-talkies, we brought them as a joke to use at the dance. We expect to create a sensation. Talk it up. Laugh. Act puzzled at the delay—"

Some cars, after being halted, were waved on; others were being sent to a side street for further inspection. The assemblage of police, highway patrolmen and sheriff's deputies looked very imposing.

In the Cadillac elderly gaiety reigned. "Who's Juan Fangio?" Biff said.

"The greatest race driver who ever lived," Bill said. "I mean, until this darling girl at my left came along."

"She's Juana Fangio," Sid said.

They all laughed. Brenda stopped. A huge, helmeted man in khaki leaned in her window and ran a powerful flashlight over them. He smiled.

"All dressed up, aren't you, folks?" he said.

"We're going to the ball," Brenda said. "The one at Golden Years. And we're already late."

"It's a long trip from Laguna," Carter said. "And the traffic is terrible on Saturday nights."

"We shouldn't have stopped for a drink," Bill said.

"Don't say that in front of a policeman!" Brenda snapped.

The cop smiled again. "Well, it was just one, wasn't it?"

"At our age," Biff said, "we can't handle more than one. Honest."

They giggled nervously. Sweat was gathering on Biff's countenance.

"Is something the matter, officer?" Sid asked. "Should we go home?"

"Oh, no," the cop said benevolently. "Go have some fun at the dance." He waved his hand and stepped back. "Something is always wrong, more or less, you know."

Brenda drove on. There was a long silence, broken only by labored breathing. Carter, spent and feeling very aged, reflected that probably his interest in geriatrics was the sole reason he was still around. But his arthritis was kicking up, he had abdominal pains from agitatedly gulping air, his head throbbed from eye strain, and he calculated his blood pressure at about 190 systolic. And he could see the others were hardly better off. What a hell of a bunch of bank robbers!

"There's one thing about being a senior citizen," Bill remarked. "The fuzz are nice to you. . . ."

In Dr. Tilden's house they had time for only a hasty examination of the loot. It consisted of two hundred forty thousand dollars in bills of large denomination, and was put in cellophane bags and hidden in the vegetable crisping tray in the refrigerator. The radios and guns were dropped into an empty carton, covered by a layer of newspapers, and left in the garage. Everybody but Brenda and Carter wanted to go to bed.

"Impossible," Carter decreed, and pulled on his mask. "We're not in the clear by any means, and we've got to do everything to avoid suspicion. We're going to be the life of the party and act drunk and stay up till dawn. Understand?"

They understood and called upon the last of their physical reserves. None could have been faulted for his conduct at the assembly hall; they all danced and drank punch and were charming to people they hated and ate finger sandwiches. Brenda flirted, and they joined in a community sing of "Harvest Moon" and "Deep in the Heart of Texas" and stayed until the exhausted band played "Good Night, Ladies." All of them, frenetically revived, looked for Grover T. Gaston, but he wasn't to be found. Somebody said he had refused to attend because liquor was not served.

"I wish he'd come," Brenda confided to Sid. "I'd have let him have a pinch or two for that kind of money. It would have been a pleasant feeling."

"I have no feeling at all," Sid replied. "Especially in my feet." She shook her head. "Never again."

They separated at dawn, heading for Snug Harbor and Sunset Town and Safe Haven and Journey's End respectively, more dead than alive. Although the musicians had been instructed, as usual, to furnish safe and slow numbers, several revelers were authentically dead —three men, including a popular bachelor who had gone down forever at his fiancée's feet, and one overweight old wife. That news took precedence in Golden Years over the night of outlawry on the south coast.

A faint, pleasing glow gradually animated the Seniles, despite twinges of apprehension, persistent fatigue and aching joints. Their latest feats attracted more attention than they were really prepared for, and of course they could take no credit for them except among themselves.

The authorities moved ponderously, the intervening Sunday occasioned a delay, and so the story gathered and maintained momentum. It took a little while for the cops to connect the clobbering of the power substation with the destruction at the bank. Witnesses had clearly seen armed hippies cutting off the lights, and at first the deed was assumed to be another outrage on the part of Black Panthers, the SDS, or others. Then the tie-up with the wrecked Yachtsmen's branch was established. And it was a wreck—scenes on television graphically illustrated what Sam and his Hispano-Suiza cannon had done. Because Frontier was part of the national banking system, the Federal Bureau of Investigation entered the case.

Returns continued to come in for nearly a week.

The Corvette was found, the Pontiac, the school bus. By a coincidence that charmed the Seniles, Biff had stowed abandoned clothing in the same park trash can Bill had used, and this attire was duly discovered. More witnesses came forward: the sailors, a parking lot attendant who remembered an old guy with a moustache in a new Corvette he couldn't drive, people who had seen bits and pieces of the action from windows and doorways and cars, and a householder who had taken note of a new Cadillac which floated around in his neighborhood for a long time that night. But nobody had a license number for the Cadillac, and the other cars and the bus presumably employed by the bandits had been stolen.

Nothing made much sense in the investigation, including queer costumes and rapid changes and differing testimony on the ages of the participants. A highway patrolman and sheriff's deputies remembered stopping several cars containing elderly types in ball dress at a roadblock, but that was not regarded as especially significant.

Whether the ball at Golden Years was an important factor remained obscure. Unquestionably the robbers had employed the occasion as a cover for escape. But other far more puzzling factors took precedence.

There was no doubt that at least two women had been involved, indeed a novelty in bank robberies. This prompted a newspaper headline: GRANDMA BANDIT STRIKES IN VAIN! The agent in charge of the local FBI office stated that he doubted the existence of any "Grandma Bandit" and considered the raid on the Yachtsmen's branch the work of an experienced and highly professional outfit which specialized in bewildering disguises. In reply to a question, he said he had yet to be convinced the bank job had anything in common with the big Palm Springs jewel robbery (outside the bureau's jurisdiction) except that, according to witnesses, elderly people had worked in both felonies.

So far, lacking anything approaching a definite identification, nothing concrete could be concluded. His own
impression was that eastern criminals were involved,
all new to California, and that no doubt they were far
away by now. When a reporter wondered if the crooks
could be quartered in Golden Years, the spokesman
laughed and said he wished it was that easy.

Obviously the robbery, ingeniously planned and ex-
ecuted, had been a failure. Using their rapid-fire
antitank gun, the police theorized, the gang had got
into the vault and then run out of time while attempting to open the strong room; probably the lights coming back on had forced them to flee in the bus. Their
whereabouts for a brief period afterward were trace-
able: the pair in the sports car had eluded pursuit, and
the confederates who had smashed the bank went to
hide in the park comfort station. Whether the man in
the Cadillac had been their wheelman was a matter of
conjecture. Those luxury cars were very common in
Southern California. The reason for suspecting it was
the getaway car—and here the local cops didn't agree
with the FBI—lay in the fact that such a vehicle figured in the Palm Springs job, and that aspect couldn't
be ruled out.

A new element was injected when a couple of radio
hams and one or more governmental short-wave stations
reported hearing faint, mystifying signals in a kind of
code which hinted the robbers had coordinated their
efforts through the use of portable transmitters. The
names "Able" and "Charley" were picked up, and
transmissions mentioning the fuzz and Padre Serra Park.

"Oh, boy," Sam said. "That was the crucial moment.
I can't tell you how I hated to send our location in the
clear. But I couldn't think of anything else. If one of
those guys had known what to do with what he was listening to, we would have been goners."

The group waited for the discovery of the automatic
cannon. Sam had bought it while living in Texas, had

had it sent express; the company in Chicago he had dealt with was now out of business, and he had filed identifying numbers off the weapon; but still tracing was possible. Nothing like that happened. Buried in a welter of interviewing witnesses, and quite a few nuts who fancied they could help, as well as dusting for fingerprints and taking casts of footprints, and perhaps with an eagerness vitiated by the fact that no money was missing, the police did not search in the ocean. Nobody went swimming off the bank point, which was rocky and untrustworthy because of erratic tides. Sam's cannon remained undisturbed, no doubt sunk in the bottom ooze and gathering barnacles, well hidden by polluted coastal waters.

"I don't like losing the piece," Sam said, in time. "I'm almost disposed to go back some night and pick it up."

He perceived instantly that he wasn't going to have any company.

What with colonial wars, rack and ruin in Academe, and bitter black aspirations, the case rapidly vanished from the public scene. A pair of courteous men in plain clothes, carrying badges, did come to Golden Years and asked questions of the personnel at the administrative center. They found no leads. Half the residents of Snug Harbor owned new Cadillacs. There were some gun buffs in the community, like Sam, but no one had ever heard of an antitank cannon or an antiaircraft pompom of the kind the cops were looking for. And tracing the movements of masked individuals on the night of the annual madness of the ball was patently impossible. The investigators politely thanked their informants and went away. Although Golden Years was notably a place for gossip and sensation, the questioning failed to titillate the general fancy. That senior citizens with a bent for crime were among them was just too ridiculous for serious consideration.

The FBI said its investigation was continuing and that the files were never closed until apprehension and conviction had been achieved.

One curious incident, scarcely noted except at the Snug Harbor country club, closed the proceedings. Even this was mere hearsay, and concerned Grover T. Gaston. He had gone to the Yachtsmen's branch when it was repaired and again open for business, the story went, transacted a few matters, and opened his safe deposit box. Then something incredible happened. Grover allegedly cursed, cried and grew maniacal. Mr. Cooper, the assistant manager, was forced to call a doctor to calm the old boy. He claimed his box had been looted, that he had lost everything—his birth certificate, Army discharge papers, stocks and bonds, and other valuables. Nothing he mentioned seemed irreplaceable, and Mr. Cooper tried vainly to reason with him, pointing out that such a robbery was impossible and nearly as absurd as Grover's assertion that the goddam robbers had been after him alone. Thereupon Grover attempted to assault him. Police joined the doctor and Grover was taken away in custody. In truth, his box was empty, but the assumption was that Gaston, in an unstable mental state, had probably removed his papers on a previous occasion and lost them when his yacht was ransacked. The blow on the head he had received during that raid undoubtedly explained his present incoherence and delusions.

Grover's ex-wife happily furnished the end of the tale. He was now in a rest home, in the throes of a complete mental and physical collapse diagnosed as senile dementia by at least one physician. Since he was a veteran of World War I—having been, according to the former Mrs. Gaston, a clerk in the adjutant's office in Camp Lee, Virginia—consideration was being given to transferring him to a veterans' hospital for electrical shock treatments. The old thief was lying, she said, right up to what she hoped was the end.

Equipped with an imposing prosthetic back device (into the pads and hollow tubing of which he had stuffed Grover's life savings), Carter left on an ostensible business trip to Portland, Oregon. Brenda drove him to the international airport in Los Angeles, and he went into a toilet and put on the device. Then he boarded a Scandinavian Airlines System jet for Copenhagen, and changed there to a plane for Zurich. Everyone was helpful and sympathetic toward the severely handicapped old gentleman hurrying to Switzerland for medical aid, including customs men.

Carter spent two hours in Zurich, unloading his device and making a deposit at the Grundich et Cie Bank that didn't raise an eyebrow. Another jet took him to London and New York; in the latter airport he waited an hour, and then he enjoyed a new movie en route to Los Angeles. He was gone a total of thirty-seven and a half hours.

"The wages of sin are bankable," he told his associates at the champagne party they gave for him upon his return. "Put that down in your notebooks. But I think I've had enough."

"Amen," Biff said.

XXXXXXX WITHIN A MONTH the gang was at it again. They knew they shouldn't be—they were still tired from the last job, they were rich, and obviously a perfectly planned operation was beyond their capabilities. And the law of probabilities guaranteed that sooner or later they would blow a job.

But they were more restless than ever. The onset of autumn was hot and made them irritable. A combination of opportunity and their prejudices was terribly inviting.

Bill Canary initiated the project. One night at a gathering at Major Crawford's, Bill insisted they watch on the major's color television set a special variety show which featured Dow Jones and the Four Averages. Everybody grumbled; they detested nearly all young people and their folk heroes, and especially those who wore outlandish costumes and played electric guitars and wailed songs of misery and protest. Among them was some commiseration for Negro youth, but not much. On the whole, they regarded the latest generation as cowards, freaks, crybabies, immoralists, drug addicts, pampered fools and downright villains. They often longed to get even with the little bastards.

Dow Jones (formerly Ferd Issogonik) was smallish, rounded, dimpled, wide-eyed, wide-mouthed and presumably male, with long black hair that fell in dense

"**Madge! A dishwashing liquid to soften hands?**"

"Relax. It's <u>Palmolive.</u> Softens hands while you do dishes."

If you're getting enough stimulation from this book, you don't need it from your coffee.

Sanka® Decaffeinated Coffee is the good-tasting coffee that is 97% caffein-free, so it won't add to your days. Or your nights, either.

disarray to the shoulders of the black suits—with bell-bottom pants—and the collars of the purple shirts he wore. He affected plug hats of silk, startling wide white cravats, sometimes a sash around his waist, half boots of patent leather, and huge dark glasses. During the course of his performances he shouted harshly like a movie Apache attacking a wagon train, sang whisper-ingly, bellowed, groaned orgiastically, and in romantic moods attained a clear soprano, all the while pounding his plugged-in instrument. Also Dow Jones danced—a sort of combined strut and Tokyo university student quickstep, varied by Nijinsky leaps—and behind him swayed and moaned the Four Averages, beating on electrified devices and pounding drums and shaking maracas. The Averages were somewhere between male and female in guise, running in size from large to small and from fat to lean, incredibly scruffy and bearded and spangled, and plug-hatted. Dow, as he preferred to be called, had only a wispy snit on his chin and side-burns which ran to the verges of his jaws.

Most of his material he furnished himself, although he couldn't read music. He was the author of "Big-Butted Baby" and "Napalm Love," as well as several other best-selling records and albums. His rise to suc-cess and riches in the past couple of years had been incredibly swift. Often he improvised on the spot, en-couraged by the mad enthusiasm of his contemporaries. Underground newspaper critics said he was sidereal, man, a funky, swingy singer, outstanding, backed by a wild blues-rock outfit that had somehow been given a shot of speed by classical jazz. When he did "Lay Me Down on Fillmore Street" he killed them dead.

Fortress Recordings, Incorporated, had signed Dow to a five-year, two-million-dollar contract. This coming winter he would headline in a series of six television spectaculars. His one-night stands across country brought in from fifteen to twenty thousand dollars per engagement. A Las Vegas hotel was reputedly offering a hundred thousand dollars for a single week. Touring Europe had been an unbroken series of triumphs, even in some of the socialist republics; no matter where he and the Averages went, they were dug. Nothing could better attest to his fame and fortune than the fact that he was guided by Management Associates Cartel (MAC to the entertainment industry), an almighty worldwide agency which represented only those artists who promised to reap millions. Dow was MAC's current pick of the litter. He was under the personal management of the president, Mr. Mort Zimbal. Movie columnists had said he would soon do a picture with nude scenes in it.

The Seniles sat and looked and listened grimly while Bill filled them in on Dow and company. Bill's purpose evaded them. Getting up irritably, Sam turned off the television set.

"I can't bear that noise," he said.

"This is the end," Carter said. "Organized groups of sodomists howling at the moon and being paid for it. Our nation can't last much longer."

"I played a girl in a hobo jungle in a depression movie," Sidney Ellen said, "and we had better wardrobes than that."

"I think *he's* rather cute," Bill ventured.

Sam glared at him. "Do you? Well, I don't. He and his audiences are yellowbellies and queers, dodging the draft and taking dope and getting venereal diseases and wrecking their schools. Not one of the buggers could go out and earn a living."

"He's earning something more than a living," Bill replied.

"Yes, damn it," Sam said. "That's why America's finished, as Carter said."

"That's my point, Major."

"Huh?" Carter said.

"MAC would certainly miss him. Actually, they couldn't afford to be without Dow, could they?"

After a silence, Carter said, "No-o. Have you a suggestion you're concealing?"

Bill had one. He had been giving the matter a lot of thought. In short, he was advancing the notion that they snatch Dow Jones.

Again Carter said, "No-o." He seemed to be struggling with himself, and sighed and shook his head. "No, Bill. It's too soon. It may always be too soon for us. We have to face up to the truth—we're pretty far along, and Palm Springs and the Yachtsmen's branch were near messes. Try as we will, we just can't make these things go smoothly. Next time we'll stub our toes."

"I agree, Doctor," Biff said. "Why don't we all take our shares of the dough, get out of here, and—"

"Shut up," Sam commanded. He looked hard at Bill. "You say you've been thinking; what else have you got to offer?"

"Perhaps half a million. What is Dow worth? At least that, eh?"

"He's not worth a goddam cent—but on the other hand—"

"That's what I mean, Sam."

"Five hundred thousand?" Sid asked, and blinked.

"Why not, luv? MAC can pull that in for him in a month or two."

"I suspect kidnapping is the hardest of anything to get away with," Carter said. "The dangers are immense. The police apparently always drop everything else in order to hunt for kidnappers." He shook his head once more. "No, I'm afraid not. We aren't physically or mentally prepared for the effort."

"I agree, Doctor," Biff said. "Absolutely." He was still suffering aftershocks from that evening at the bank. "I say we've done enough, kids. Let's retire."

"Uh-huh," Sam said. "Bill, how would you take him?"

"I don't know. By the easiest means possible. Nothing fancy."

"Yeah. You make it sound simple. And how would you hold him?"

"Oh, I have an idea for that," Bill said.

He had indeed, and they listened intently. It had the merits of simplicity, ease and sheer, sparkling novelty. An almost quiescent élan revived in some of them. Brenda was amused and giggled; nothing bothered her since she had outrun the cops, and she welcomed the discussion of new schemes instead of flouncing out of the room. She had inspired in Carter a certain tolerance mildly suffused by affection, and he had promised her, when they were in the proper circumstances, not a mere Corvette but a Ferrari or a Maserati.

"Oh, I think that's lovely!" she said. "You're a genius, Bill. It sounds like fun."

"I think the idea stinks," Biff said. "Put me on record."

"Why?" Bill demanded. "Because I thought of it? Or because you're a coward?"

"Because I'm a coward," Biff retorted. "They can come in handy at times."

Sam's eyes were squinted. "How do we collect on the bum? Tell us that."

Bill shrugged. "As usual, I guess. Have the ransom paid by check. That's the businesslike way, isn't it?"

"There's an even better method," Carter said. "Have the ransomee pay for his own deliverance and you've reduced collection to its essentials."

"Great!" Sid said involuntarily. "Biff can handle the negotiations."

"Not me," Biff said.

Grimacing, Carter said: "I wish I wasn't so fertile. I honestly don't want to get involved. . . ."

"You are the genius," Sam said to Bill. "What if something goes wrong? I can't actually believe anybody would pay more than ten dollars to get the little bastard back. And remember this time, after holding him, you'll have a witness who can put the finger on all or most of us. What will you do with him?"

"Uh, that's a problem—" Bill started to say.

"Not really," Sid interjected. "We kill him. Perhaps we kill him whether he pays or not. Isn't that more or less routine in kidnappings?"

"I must confess I like her solution," Carter said.

Biff paled, stared at Sid and then at Brenda, and licked his lips; he appeared frightened and fascinated.

Brenda puffed out her lips in an expression of distaste. "That wouldn't be nice," she said.

"You wouldn't do it, would you, kid?" Biff asked.

"No," Brenda said.

"I would," Sid said.

They were all quiet for a moment.

"Well, it's a nice thought," Sam said. "But it raises another question. What about the four other bums? We can't grab everybody, and I don't care for the idea of a massacre."

"They're of no importance without Dow," Bill said. "We can forget them."

"I agree," Carter said. "I mean, I agree those other miserable creatures are not our concern. However, I don't intend to get involved—"

In the ensuing conversation he proceeded to get deeply involved.

Several elements urged the gang forward. Criminality had given them a taste for wealth. Galloping inflation in the future was bound to cut into their profits. They hated youth, and particularly youthful entertainers like Dow. Since they had tasted blood, it didn't take much to bore them now. Pride in their achievements and the fact they had a reputation to sustain influenced them. Only Biff really argued against the project. Bill's central conception seemed too good to waste, even to Carter. And it looked easy.

"There's the hitch," he kept saying. "Appearances are deceptive. We're up against the toughest job yet. It's beyond our planning capabilities. I have a feeling of fatality about this."

Nevertheless, he presided over a series of meetings. Decision was being forced on them through what they read and heard of Dow. He was currently in Los Angeles, but he would soon leave to play the lead in a movie to be made in Yugoslavia, and afterward launch another triumphal tour of the Continent; his absence would stretch into months.

Not all the Senile sessions were plenary because Biff took to absenting himself, pleading minor illnesses or saying he had to go to a driving range at night to get himself in tune for the fall golf tournament at Snug Harbor; it was quite evident he was opposed to further risk and was ducking out on them. The others discussed his apostasy, and decided he could not be excused on a number of counts; Sidney Ellen was appointed to bring him back into the fold.

She had to telephone several times before she reached him. He sounded nervous and uncertain. She said, "You'd better talk to me, Biff. I'm not kidding. We're all worried about you and your attitude."

"There's nothing to worry about. It's just that I'm not a well man—"

"Biff, don't stall me."

"Listen, you're not scaring me. This is a free country—"

"Come on. When are we going to meet? I can't wait forever."

"Tomorrow morning at the Happy Talk," he said reluctantly. "Ten o'clock. We'll have a coffee and Danish. Sid, I've got a terrible problem."

"I know," she said. "You've got a jellied backbone."

He was waiting for her next day at the cafeteria, and they picked up their food and drink and put their trays on a table remote from the other breakfasters and sat down. Biff, who had not smoked since the first lung cancer scare, surprised Sid by lighting a cigarette. The fingers that held the match trembled.

"What's this?" she asked.

"I don't care," he said. "Nothing's left for me. I can't go on."

"Because you're scared?"

"No, that's not it . . . part of it, but not the real reason."

"Well?"

He looked at her and groaned. "I'm in love, Sid, and I know it's hopeless."

Having long expected this, and not really surprised, she almost matched his groan. She stared at him, saddened by his exhibition of emotions that no longer became either of them and were somehow pitiful and revived a sense of mortal loss. He bit feverishly into his sticky pastry and talked with his mouth full.

"You wouldn't understand," he said thickly. "You've just let yourself grow old. That's the pity of it. You don't feel anything any more . . . Sid, a person doesn't have to give up."

To her dismay, she was close to tears. But he was awful—big and clumsy looking and red-eyed from drinking at the club and being in poker games, and his nose had been broken several times and had a putty texture.

"But I do understand," she said. "I do, Biff. I'm flattered." Half-forgotten movie dialogue, long outmoded, tripped on her tongue. "Only it can never be. I like you as a friend, a good companion, but my heart is not—"

"What have you got to do with it? Or your heart? I'm talking about Brenda. She's driving me nuts."

"Oh." Sid's face felt hot. She would have liked to throw her coffee in his moon face.

"Ever since I saw her in that tutu. I can't get her out

of my mind, so the best thing for me to do is stay away. I feel choked up when I see her. She's my last love."

"Oh."

"What can I do, Sid? Sooner or later it's bound to come out. And Carter is my friend. I can't do that to him. Anyway, he's got the money—he'd cut me and Brenda off without a cent."

"Does Brenda know?"

"Well, I haven't got down to cases, but I gave her a couple of squeezes at the masked ball and she wasn't exactly sore. . . . Oh, sometimes I think I ought to keep on. The doctor is a very old guy and he won't last forever. If I could keep myself under control—"

"That's right, Biff," Sid said, and detested the Borgia duplicity she had to employ. "And the more jobs he's in, the more likely he is to go under. Don't give up Brenda while you still have a chance for happiness."

"Do you really think so?"

"Cross my heart and hope to die."

"Let's not talk about dying. Or going to jail, either." Biff's eyes softened. "But maybe someday we could live in Europe or South America. I'd give her every luxury."

"Then you need more money."

"Well . . . I suppose. Will you keep my secret?"

"Certainly."

"I just might take another crack at it," Biff said, "on account of the sexiest dame in Golden Years." He smiled and patted Sid's hand. "You're a good friend, baby. You understand. You're a little too tough a bird for my taste—you make me nervous with that gun-slinging—but your heart is in the right place."

Sidney Ellen went away from him thinking, with uncharacteristic and unladylike heat, "The big fat son of a bitch!"

It was not one of her best days. Bill took the news of Biff's compliance badly; Sid did not, of course, disclose the reason.

"Who needs him?" Bill said. "I think we'd be better

off without him." He had shampooed his hair and was spraying carefully combed locks in front of a mirror in his trailer. "You know, I suddenly see myself in a different light, luv." He straightened and regarded his reflection piercingly. "As a sort of a take-charge guy. A leader. This is my idea. I ought to be in command. Where would we be without me? Do you have that feeling?"

"Oh, sure," Sid said. She swallowed her animus; but she wondered if she was getting fed up.

Another television program clinched Bill's proposal. All the Seniles except Biff and Sam had been to a widely heralded movie which depicted the association of a vague, troubled, teen-aged couple who met, took off their clothing, got into bed together, drove around, suffered, undressed, slept with each other, talked at length, and sadly endured the incomprehension and oppressions of idiot parents, teachers and other older members of the establishment; at near midnight they gathered in Sam's house for iced coffee and peanut butter sandwiches. Everybody was disgruntled. Bill turned on a late talk show. The star attraction was Dow Jones, without the Averages.

He was dressed in a long African tribal garment, sandals and beads, and played and sang a new hit, "Big Sur, Big Sir and Madam." Then he talked to the comedian whose program it was. Dow was in good form, mumbling and playful, hidden behind huge dark round glasses. His social comments were penetrating.

"I gotta speak out for the new people," he said, among other worse things. "It's like a compulsion. You know? I have to keep on these shades so they won't see I'm crying. The new people—us—they listen to me, you know. I dig revolution and black is beautiful and that area. You know? Like I'm not putting the old folks down, man." He laughed. "I don't need to, you know. Man, they're clapped out. They're already down, man. *Down!*"

A deathly stillness held Sam's living room. Carter's upper lip was peeled back, revealing the plastic pink gum of his denture, and Sam grew livid. Sid averted her eyes from the tube, feeling adrenalin speeding her heart.

"He *is* cute," Brenda said.

"I told you," Bill replied, and grinned and looked coolly around at his companions.

"Here we go . . ." Biff said faintly.

"Yes, let's go," Carter said. "Damn the torpedoes."

"I'm with you, Doctor," Sam said.

"Me too," Sid said.

"Like the future of the country is up for grabs," Dow was saying. "They need me, man—"

A plan evolved quickly. Its first implementation necessitated Sidney Ellen leaving for a vacation in Arizona, and Bill going on holiday in San Francisco. They didn't leave on the same day, and their departures were well publicized.

Forty-eight hours later they both turned up in San Francisco, put their cars in separate storage garages, altered appearances in toilet cubicles in busy restaurants near Union Square, and separately flew back to Los Angeles. They met at a large airport hotel, registering as brother and sister and occupying adjoining rooms. Bill had rented a Chevrolet sedan from an airport agency.

His hair was now white and cut *en brosse*. He wore horn-rimmed spectacles and well-worn gray sport jacket and gray flannel slacks, he was stooped and his small belly was thrust out; he had added years.

Sid was also changed for the worse. She had pepper-and-salt hair in a generous wig that ended in a bun on the nape of her neck. Her glasses were the half-lens sort, over which she peered uncertainly. No makeup softened the lines of her countenance. She was clad in plain, unfashionable dresses that fell below her knees and sensible shoes and stockings of thick texture.

But, of course, they had become different people. They were Ethel and Rodney Smith, of Palmdale, California, and they had a sick relative off-scene. In their possession were examples of Sam's handicraft, including fake driving licenses, social security numbers and bankbooks. Carter had schooled them thoroughly in the new roles, and they liked everything about the project but the disguises.

"I'm a fright," Sid complained. "I look a hundred!"

"Look at me, for God's sake," Bill said. "My posture is terrible and I've been tailored by the A&P. You know what I am? A *clean* old man!"

Within a week they found a cavernous, ancient green house on the oceanfront in the Malibu Colony. The hardware had a scrofulous patina and was rusting, the furniture and carpets were threadbare, and the place smelled of disintegrating plumbing and seaweed and salt. From upper-story bedrooms and an attached tea-house in front, however, was a splendid view of beach and water. A constant booming of breakers and walls between the houses on either side ensured privacy. Although the high summer season was past, the rent was eight hundred dollars a month. At their expressions of horror, the realty man was moved to argue with the owner, who came down to six hundred and fifty. Sid and Bill conferred agitatedly and decided they might just be able to afford it for two months. She gave the agent thirteen hundred dollars in traveler's checks.

"This money was for a trip," she explained, "the first one ever—to Europe. But then our dear young relative got sick—" She dabbed at her eyes, easily summoning tears. "Well, maybe we can go someday."

"The main thing is for the kid to have rest and quiet," Bill said.

"This is an ideal spot for you," the agent said. "The

guy to your south has moved back into town since school started and only brings his family down weekends; the house on the north belongs to an actress and she's away in England making a picture—her boyfriend is there with a maid, but he isn't around much. The Colony is fenced and patrolled by guards. You couldn't find greater privacy."

"I know we're going to be happy and safe here," Sid said.

The agent was touched by her timidity and by how she gazed at him appealingly over her reading glasses. He didn't bother to raise the issue of the Smiths posting a five-hundred-dollar deposit against damages to the premises—they were obviously trustworthy.

Bill brought in cartons and suitcases for the benefit of the curious, and Sid went on foot to the nearby market to buy supplies. She made the acquaintance of the movie actress's maid next door, Golda by name, a blowsy old party with lavender hair and a prying manner. Miss Anita Gallo was the actress, and she had left in Golda's care her dog named Harvey—an aged German shepherd whose frosty green eyes and grizzled muzzle bespoke his years. Every day Golda walked Harvey. She said the boyfriend of Miss Gallo hardly ever came home and was running around with other women. The Smiths plainly engrossed her.

Sid took a liking to Harvey, but Golda worried her. She sent off a postcard to Dr. Tilden reading: "Having a wonderful time, wish you were here. Beach lovely. Ever, Ethel." That was part of their prearranged code, and in due course, from the market at Malibu, she dialed the number of another public booth in the community center at Golden Years. Carter answered. She detailed the Colony setup and mentioned the nosy maid.

"Is she apt to present a problem?" he asked.

"I think I can handle her."

"Ummmm. Well, we can always call it off if she is

[132]

troublesome. We may have to anyhow. The map Brenda got to the movie stars' homes in Bel Air— that's where Jones lives—is correct. But she and Biff have had trouble in observation. The place is walled and has a locked gate. There is a big dog who runs loose and barks. It is difficult to tell when Jones is home. We can't seem to obtain his unlisted telephone number, which has been changed several times. I have abandoned the idea of our attempting to get in by posing as gardeners or repairmen; I just don't think it will wash, that his servants will fall for it. On the other hand, there is no point to our forcing entrance in a holdup and then finding Jones is not present. Biff and Brenda dare not turn up in the neighborhood too often, so Sam and I are taking up their duties. However, I'm afraid keeping an eye on the house is not going to suffice. We will have to have more reliable information."

"Can't you pick him up in his car?"

"Very dangerous and impractical."

"Shall I try our alternate approach?" she said.

"It's worth a try, I suppose," he said. "If you develop anything, call me at the country club tomorrow noon and have me paged."

Going north on the highway to Trancas, Sid entered a telephone booth in a restaurant and called Management Associates Cartel in Hollywood, employing a sprightly clubwoman's accents honed in a number of minor movie parts. Asking for Mr. Mort Zimbal did no good. She had to explain her purpose to successive haughty secretaries. As she put more coins in the box, she was switched to a Mr. Denny Goodman, in charge of publicity.

"I'm Mrs. Florabelle Nevins, Mr. Goodman," she said, "chairwoman of the program committee of the Friends of the Music Center. We are preparing our winter program of concerts in the Dorothy B. Chandler Pavilion. I'm sure you have heard of our organization

—it represents all of the advanced music lovers in the city."

"Oh, yes, Mrs. Nevins."

"Many of our children and grandchildren seem to adore a young man I believe you manage, Mr. Dow Jones."

"That's right, Mrs. Nevins."

Sid laughed. "Mr. Goodman, we're determined not to become old fogies in our group. That's why we would like to have Mr. Jones do a concert for us."

"Dow?" Goodman said. "At the Music Center?" His gulp was audible. "Why, that's a kind of an exciting thought, Mrs. Nevins."

"I hope so. We could give him a royal welcome."

"It's a prestige item—a new gig for him. I could run it up on the flagpole here and see if anybody salutes. . . . But, Mrs. Nevins, you know Dow's type of music—"

"Oh, yes," Sid said. "That doesn't matter. It would be a *surprise* for the Friends, something new."

"Uh-huh."

"But I'd need to see Mr. Jones, talk to him, before we entered negotiations and made an announcement. We must agree on things."

"Yeah," Goodman said. "Well—"

"Naturally he'd have to do some standards— 'Trees,' 'The Road to Mandalay'—and so forth."

"Yes. Really? Well—"

"Our membership, you know. Old ones as well as young ones. But I flatter myself our sponsorship could do a lot for Mr. Jones."

"Sure. Well—"

"When may I see him to talk this over? Time is of the essence, Mr. Goodman. I am going to Europe next week to engage European artists."

"Mrs. Nevins, I couldn't say right off the cuff. I've got to take a few soundings here and alert Mr. Zimbal. Where can I get back to you?"

Sid gave him a phony telephone number, and hope fled her. "I'd so hoped we could come to a quick decision on this. I want to present something to the committee at once. Wouldn't Mr. Jones be available during one of the next two or three evenings? Might he drop by my house? I live in Bel Air."

"I'm afraid not," Goodman said. "Dow works nights with the Averages. He's got a complete recording studio in his house. His hours are irregular like most artists, Mrs. Nevins. Every morning he's up and on a health kick, building up the body for a movie he's going to do." He chuckled. "You know how they always take off their clothes in them now."

"Perhaps you can give me his telephone number and I can ring him."

"I wish I could, but I can't. The kids, all his admirers, drive him crazy on the horn. He has to keep changing his number."

"I see. Well, I suppose we'd better forget this—"

"No, no. Wait a minute. I'll ramrod this through and get you a quick answer. I like the gig myself. Maybe we can meet Dow when he jogs down Stone Canyon to Sunset Boulevard and back. That's each day. We might stop him at the Bel Air Hotel for a minute or two. Could you show up on short notice, Mrs. Nevins?"

"Certainly."

"Okay. I'll get through to you soonest. Thanks for your interest."

"Thank you, Mr. Goodman," Sid said, from the bottom of her heart.

She went back and conferred with Bill. They regarded one another raptly.

"The opportunity of a lifetime," he pronounced. "It's falling into our laps."

"Carter won't like just rushing in," she said.

"Oh, phooey. He's too cautious."

"Maybe you'd better talk to him."

"All right. Give me the car keys."

When Bill had gone, Sid took a walk on the beach. It was deserted under a lowering sky, and a stiff onshore wind blew showers of spray off the breaking waves. Anticipating the early arrival of Dow made her very nervous. As she returned, Golda came from next door leading Harvey on a leash.

"We were watching for you," she said. "Harv barked when you went out."

Sid knelt to pet the dog, who sat down composedly and licked her hand. She envied him his calm.

"When's your sick relative coming?" Golda asked.

"How did you know about that?"

"Honey, I talk to everyone. I got it from the day gateman. He keeps the Colony up on all the latest news. I guess he got it from your real estate agent."

"Oh . . . yes."

"Is it a him or a her?"

"Our niece," Sid said. "She's the daughter of our youngest sister, who died with her husband in an auto accident a few years ago. Rodney and I are very fond of her."

"What's her name?"

"Ernestine Potts."

"Pretty first name," Golda said. "I don't care for the Potts part, though. You ought to change it to Smith." She grinned. "That's a common name you got, Ethel, but it's better than Potts."

"Well, she can change her name when she marries."

"Is she going steady with anybody?"

"Not now, no."

"What's the matter with her?"

"Ernestine has a heart condition," Sid said. "She lives in Palmdale, in the desert, and the summer heat has weakened her. The doctor ordered a rest in a cooler climate."

"Who's she live with in Palmdale?"

"Uh, another sister who is married."

"Who's her doctor?"

"Dr. Morton, Frederick Morton. He's our family physician."

"What grade is Ernestine in?"

Advance planning had not taken into account the presence of a Golda; the rapid extemporizing demanded of Sid rattled and irritated her. She knew some of these snap replies would be difficult to remember.

"She's a senior in Palmdale High," Sid said, "and a little behind because she has had to drop out several times."

"I used to practical nurse," Golda said. "I had a few heart patients. I'll be glad to help you take care of her, honey. No charge."

"Oh, thank you very much, but Rod and I can manage." Sid scrambled to her feet, getting sand in her shoes. "Golda, I have to go, really."

Harvey barked at the fleeing Sid.

"That's a funny thing," Golda called. "Old Harv is gone on you, Ethel. He barks now every time he sees you or thinks he hears you."

Behind a locked door, Sid stopped to consider. She feared even Harvey was after her. And amid the smells of an imperfect cesspool and the constant sea, she thought she detected the odor of nemesis, which would be Golda.

Every Wednesday afternoon Carter went to the physical therapy unit of Golden Years for a swirl-bath, steam and massage. He hated to be disturbed during these sessions, which soothed and restored him, and his annoyance was evident when, on the rubbing table, the attendant had to answer the telephone and returned to say the call was for him.

"Who is it?" he asked testily. "Can't it wait?"

"The lady says it's urgent."

Draping a towel around his middle, Carter went into an anteroom. "Dr. Tilden," he said.

"Rodney," Bill said in the same high voice he had used with the masseur.

"What's the matter?"

Bill told him. Carter took note of signs of increasing blood pressure.

"See here," he said. "You're asking us to pick up the merchandise in broad daylight on a public thoroughfare at a time not specified in advance. It's bad business."

"We can't chicken out now, Carter."

"Indeed we can!"

"What do you mean?" Bill said hotly. "After Sid has hit the jackpot? Are you crazy?"

"No, you are. I'll call you tonight when I have thought it over—" Someone came into the anteroom behind Carter's back. "Very well, my dear. Take two aspirins and lie down. Let me know if you have any other symptoms."

"Yes, luv."

The remainder of the rub had been spoiled for Carter. As he walked outside to wait for Brenda to pick him up an arthritic heat in his knees gave him a stiff gait; he presumed the manifestation was psychosomatic and pondered on why the hell he punished himself in this fashion during his last days on earth. Brenda was late, as usual, and the rear seat of the Cadillac was strewn with her purchases. He countermanded their normal martinis and luncheon at the country club and ordered her to go home.

"Carty," she said. "Are you hurting?"

"Dying," he said. "Slowly and painfully."

While she prepared sandwiches, he summoned Sam and Biff, who were difficult to reach and late in arriving. All of them ate lettuce and tomato on toast and drank nonfat milk and listened to the news. They did not seem to share his alarm and looked fatuously eager, which provoked his anger.

"We're off on the wrong foot already," he concluded, "and forced into improvisation."

"It looks feasible to me," Sam said. "We pick up the little bastard and stash him away. What else did you have in mind, Carter?"

"We're taking too many risks. Daylight kidnapping on the street is bad enough, God knows—if you're willing to assume Goodman has given correct information. But there's more. We have no exact time on Jones; we may have to wait the whole morning before he appears, with all the attendant dangers. Who knows how unsophisticated Goodman is? He may have already called the Friends of the Music Center to check on Mrs. Nevins before he goes further with his arrangements."

"We can't have everything our own way."

"No—and we can proceed to put our head in the noose when we haven't. Sid exceeded her instructions in talking to him. I don't like any of us acting on our own. She was not supposed to press for a time or to bring things to a head, only to somehow acquire a telephone number we could use under various pretenses to establish when Jones was home and available to us."

"But she found what we needed to know, didn't she?" Sam said. "And got us a big break in the bargain. I think we ought to take advantage of it. I don't think Goodman finding out that Mrs. Nevins isn't what she represented herself to be is a deterrent. Apparently somebody is always trying to meet that little bastard, and she could be just another mad admirer. Why or how could Goodman ever jump to the conclusion that talking to some foolish woman was the preliminary to a kidnapping?"

"And if Jones doesn't happen to jog tomorrow morning?"

"We'll have lost a day. We can come back the next morning—and the morning after that. I'll give you a bet, and furnish good odds, that Goodman will never suspect anything more than that he's been hoaxed. I don't mind waiting around for the punk, and I'm not afraid of a daylight snatch under the right conditions. If they're not right, we'll pass and try again. At least we can see what we're doing, which we can't do at night."

Carter shrugged and spread his palms upward. "Very well. Believe what you want. But I'm still opposed to it."

"Well, I vote we go tomorrow," Sam said.

"All systems are go for me," Brenda said, and smiled.

Waiting for Biff, anticipating deadlock and delay, already determined Bill and Sid wouldn't be consulted in this crisis, Carter noticed Brenda had Biff's attention.

"You don't look well, Carter," he said.

"How could I?" Carter snarled. "The least I'll incur from one of these cockamamie excursions is a coronary occlusion. What do you say?"

"Let's go," Biff said.

The remainder of the day was spent in organizing. That evening Brenda drove Biff to Los Angeles International Airport and he shopped among the rental car agencies until he found a spanking new Thunderbird he said he needed for his daughter's wedding; he was wearing a toupee and small bristling moustache and felt no need to allege that it was his granddaughter. For identification he used a false driving license Sam had prepared for him that did not bear a picture, and put down a cash deposit. Brenda followed him to a marina off Washington Boulevard and stood watch in an empty parking area for boat owners while he removed the license plates and pasted on a temporary license strip. Then they parted, Biff to take the Thunderbird to a hotel garage in Long Beach and return to Golden Years by cab, and Brenda to call Sid and Bill and go home.

Sidney Ellen picked up the wall telephone in the kitchen where she was preparing tea for herself and Bill. "Miss Smith speaking," she said.

"Aunt Ethel," Brenda said, "this is your niece."

"Yes, dear. How are you?"

"Well, pretty weak. I'm coming to stay with you tomorrow, I hope."

"That's wonderful. Rodney and I will look forward to it. I'll tell the man at the gate to pass you through. Please be careful not to overdo tomorrow, Ernestine."

"I won't, Aunt Ethel."

Sid went into the living room. Huddled in a mouldy chair, Bill stared up at her.

"It's on, Bill."

"That damn dog has been barking," he said uneasily. "He must have heard your voice. How can he hear over the waves?"

"Because he's outside, close to the house. I suppose Golda's walking him."

"She may have to go."

"Quite possibly," Sid said, and thought of the silenced pistol lying under her lingerie in a drawer upstairs.

Bill continued to stare at her, exhibiting a certain dread.

Breakfast was at five o'clock at Sam's. Sam, Carter and Brenda huddled in the kitchen under the overhead lights, pallid and wrinkled, drinking black coffee and checking out equipment. Sam handed Biff the Walther and put his service automatic in the waistband of his trousers. Even Brenda was not very sprightly, although she looked forward to driving the new Thunderbird. As on previous occasions, nervousness possessed them until Carter distributed happiness pills and gave Sam additional capsules for their quarry. Other than Carter, who wore a business suit, they were in outdoor clothing suitable to the fishing trip they had mentioned to neighbors and friends. Biff had a collection of fishing gear to load into the Cadillac as the sun brightened the sky.

"Don't look so gloomy, Carty," Brenda said.

"I'll look any way I please," he snapped. He requested them to set their watches by his, briefly rehearsed projected movements and emergency alternates, and added, "Take care of yourselves." With an awkward jerkiness, he kissed his wife. She appeared surprised and pleased, and gazed at him fondly. Biff turned away.

"Move out," Sam ordered.

Carter drove them slowly to Long Beach, condescending only to wave at their parting, and headed south. Brenda and Sam waited in mid-block, laden with equipment, until Biff arrived in the rental car; she took the wheel, Biff sat beside her, and Sam occupied the rear seat. Their pace was rapid on a lightly trafficked freeway and the surface streets. There was little conversation. Notwithstanding Carter's potions, they were keyed up. Rubbing his gnarled, liver-spotted hands, Sam studied them and decided this wasn't a hell of a lot different from testing an experimental mortar on the range at Aberdeen and getting a misfire.

Brenda turned into the pretty, wooded canyon with its handsome houses. No residents were up and about. A man in a small car was throwing folded newspapers into driveways. Near the end of the road, beside the fenced grounds of a reservoir, Brenda swung around. They passed a milk truck, and then a sallow-faced individual in the black jacket of a houseman glumly inspecting the morning and a front garden and scratching himself. The hotel parking lot was silent and devoid of movement.

"Well?" Brenda asked.

"Let's take a ride," Sam said. "The bum would never be up at this hour."

Biff nodded; he was a shade of soft saffron. "We'll be lucky to meet him by noon."

They rode aimlessly. At last Sam told Brenda to go back. Biff said hopefully that if it grew too late and things got active, of course they'd have to throw in the sponge. He received no answer and coughed and lit a cigarette.

Stone Canyon Road was more active now. Four cars, all outward bound, went by, and a Department of Water and Power truck came the other way. A shapely young woman in tight pants wheeled a pair of babies, and an enormous St. Bernard, attached to the pram on a long leash, ambled flatfootedly behind her.

"Say, look at the dog!" Brenda exclaimed. "Or is it a horse?"

"Watch your driving," Sam said. "You don't have to point out the sights to us."

"Well, I wouldn't mind living in Bel Air," she said. "It's a nice neighborhood. You probably don't meet crooks here, either."

An old gentleman, pasty and thin, walked briskly on the edge of the paving, swinging a stick—no doubt on doctor's orders. But he wasn't Dow Jones. Once more they were approaching the reservoir.

"We haven't got a prayer," Biff said. "I knew Bill and Sid would blow it."

A moment later a small, fat figure hove in view, slogging ahead, elbows pumping, attired in a large straw hat, immense dark glasses, baggy gray sweatshirt and sneakers. Sam grunted happily.

"Target!" he said. "Put on helmets." He peered up and down the road. "Clear. Cut him off, Brenda."

They pulled on motorcycle crash helmets and lowered tinted plastic face shields. Swerving to the left, Brenda blocked off Dow Jones against a hedge. Astonished and alarmed, he stared open-mouthed. Sam opened the rear door on Dow's side, covered him with the .45, grabbed him by the slack of his shirt, and jerked him into the car. Brenda slammed the door with her left hand and gunned for the right lane.

Immediately two cars passed them, headed in the opposite direction; the timing was extremely close and stupefyingly fortunate; their occupants saw nothing untoward because Sam had rapped Dow on the shoulder with the gun muzzle and forced him to the floor. He snatched off the straw hat. Dow's long locks, piled up and held partially by bobby pins, cascaded downward.

"It's him," Sam said. "Get the hell out of here." He moved away from Dow, thumb on the cocked hammer of the automatic. "Make a move, you little bastard, and they'll have to gather up your brains with a spoon."

Watching the terrible, vindictive old man, Dow cowered, his mouth still open.

Brenda reversed direction at the reservoir again and raced down the canyon. Her speed did not attract attention; all the indigenes apparently drove fast. At the first through street, just below the hotel, she turned west and followed winding, untraveled roads into the hills.

As Biff had foreseen, the design of the Thunderbird was particularly good for their purposes; it had no rear quarter-windows, and crouching occupants of the back seat were invisible from outside. Sam was already at work on Dow. He uncorked a Thermos bottle of water, produced pills, and thrust the bottle into Dow's hand; his other hand received the pills. Biff's fingers clenched in Dow's hair, restraining him.

"Hey, man . . ." Dow said. "What is this?"

"Take your medicine," Biff said. "It won't hurt you."

He took the pills and put them in Dow's mouth. Dow swallowed and gagged on them; his head jerked back. Sam rapped him on the head with the pistol and he drank more water.

"Follow orders and you won't get killed," Sam said. "Keep down. Take off your clothes."

"My clothes? Listen, all I got on underneath is a jockstrap."

"Take 'em off!"

Removing his shoes and socks, Dow eased out of the

sweatshirt. Biff had ready a frilly long nightgown, a pink robe, a voluminous blond wig, slippers. Dow experienced difficulty with the slippers; his feet were big for his size.

"You're putting me in drag—" he commented wonderingly. He was beginning to beam in a dreamy fashion.

"Lean toward me but stay on your knees," Biff told him.

Perched on the cushion, leaning back over the front seat, he grabbed Dow's hair again and applied a battery-powered razor to his jaws. The chinwhiskers and sideburns disappeared.

"You're making me straight man," Dow said. He tried to laugh.

They reached the top of the hills, with a view of the San Fernando Valley and the sea. Brenda rolled into a developing subdivision, at this hour empty of workmen, and stopped the car. She squirmed from under the wheel, leaving the engine running, turned, and accepted the makeup box Biff held ready for her.

"Hold still," she said. "I'm going to make you pretty."

"Man, this is wild," Dow said. "You know?"

His eyebrows were smoothed and extended, his cheeks given the pallor of powder, dark hollows of illness sketched under his eyes, lipstick applied. Brenda went hurriedly back to driving.

"How do I look?" Dow asked. "Like a real chick?" His head wobbled.

Biff boosted him on the seat. "Sit up like a little lady. But don't move around."

"Hey, what was in the gum drops?" Dow said. "I feel great, man! I'm flying solo!"

He collapsed. Sam wedged him in the corner and draped a shawl over his head. Crash helmets were off before his eyes were fully closed. Discarding his windbreaker, Biff put on a white jacket, gummed a brown toupee to his bald head, and adjusted steel-rimmed glasses. Brenda tilted the rear vision mirror, inspected Dow in it, and smiled.

"It sure makes you think," she said. "He's twice as cute as he was."

"Watch what you're doing," Sam growled. "Head for the barn."

He thought Dow was a miserable, puffy little creep in or out of clothing.

At the rendezvous in Topanga Canyon, Carter was out of his Cadillac, map in hand, making notes—a realty man or prospective purchaser studying the lay of the land, moustached, minus glasses and with a bushy mane of white hair. He was plainly surprised by the promptness of the task force, but there was no jubilation or any conversation exchanged beyond a few words by Sam concerning the snatch. Making certain they were unobserved, Biff took the wheel of the Thunderbird; Brenda and Sam transferred to the other car, bearing their equipment. Carter assumed Sam's place beside Dow, checked his pulse, and didn't bother to ask Biff for the pistol. Both automobiles drove off immediately, one inland and the other seaward.

On the coast highway, Biff went north to the Malibu Colony, was informed by the guard at the gate that the Smiths were expecting them, and made his way to the indicated house. A grubby woman holding an old dog on a leash promptly materialized and watched them. Although unable to see clearly without his glasses, Carter glared at her.

"Easy with Miss Potts, please, George," he said.

"Yes, Doctor," Biff replied.

He gathered Dow in his arms, taking care not to knock off the shawl or wig, and carried him inside. Carter closed the doors of the car and then stumbled over a step at the gate.

"That's Ernestine, huh?" the woman said. "The niece."

Carter didn't reply.

"You're Dr. Morton, I guess."

"Yes."

"How is she, Doctor?"

"I never discuss the condition of my patients with strangers," Carter said, and walked on.

Going inside, he closed and locked the door. He passed through the kitchen and dining room and entered the living room. The place looked gloomy and smelled abominable; all the curtains were closed. He heard voices above and faltered up the stairs, abruptly realized he was safe, and donned his glasses. His colleagues were gathered around Dow, stretched upon a bed. Although his eyes were open, he appeared comatose.

Biff gave Bill the Walther. "You won't need this. He's a little lamb."

"Why don't we just keep him this way?" Sid asked.

"Not practicable," Carter replied. "We won't risk his life. Yet." He listened to Dow's breathing. "I met the maid from next door. She worries me."

"Me too," Sid said. "I'm getting good and sick of her."

Carter bent over Dow, taking his pulse. He slapped his cheeks. "He should be more alert by now. . . . Here, you. Wake up. Pay attention to me."

Dow stirred, regarded them amiably, and sat up when Carter tugged at him. "Man, those helmets," he said. "Who got me, the senior citizens' racing team?"

"Listen, please," Carter said. "You've been kidnapped, Jones. You're being held for ransom. If you obey us, you will not be harmed. The drugs you are taking will not affect your health. You must assume another character, that of a girl. You are an invalid. Your name is Ernestine Potts. I am Dr. Morton, your physi-

[147]

cian. This woman is your aunt, Ethel Smith. Here is your uncle, Rodney Smith. Do you understand me?"

"Sure. But I'm kind of surprised. You know? Hello, Aunt Ethel and Uncle Rodney."

"Hello, Ernestine," Bill said warmly. "We want you to think of this as your temporary home."

"Thanks, Uncle Rod. Hey, Doctor, what are you charging for me?"

Carter hesitated. "We think you're worth half a million."

"Maybe more. Don't sell me short, man. I'm a big property."

"And maybe less," Carter said. "Considerably less. Or worth nothing—dead or alive. Well, that's all for the present—"

"Want to bet, Grandpaw?" Dow said.

He flailed a rigid palm into Carter's middle and sprang off the bed with incredible agility. The next instant, nightgown swishing, he administered a combined kick and chop to Bill; the Walther Bill was clutching for never emerged from his hip pocket, and he gasped and collapsed. Sid drew her automatic, but Dow smashed her right forearm with bonecracking force and sent it flying. Then he kicked her in the abdomen and she pitched under a lamp table, overturning it. From the background, Biff gazed wide-eyed at the scene: Carter lay doubled up and moaning, Bill was on his knees dazedly rubbing his numbed throat, and Sid trembled and wept underneath the lamp.

"Hey," Dow said. "You seem like a sensible old dude. I don't want to kill anybody." He extended his hands. "Look at these. They're weapons to the fuzz. You know? I'm almost a brown belt in karate. Give up, Dad?"

"You ought to be ashamed of yourself," Biff said, and advanced upon him.

"Okay," Dow said, almost in sadness. "You asked for it."

Stalking his opponent lightly, on the balls of his feet, he feinted clumsy, lurching Biff with gyrating motions and leaps, and in lightning fashion successively delivered scientific smashes from hands and elbows to the throat and body and a kick to the groin. But something was the matter; his blows and kicks were parried by Biff's big fists or arms, or brushed aside by his massive legs. Another assault was no more successful. Dow tried to seize one of Biff's hands and toss the big man over his head. It was like attempting to budge a gravel truck. Then Biff jabbed him casually in the eye. Yelping, Dow decided to leave. As he dodged, so did Biff, and Dow stopped a left hook, a straight left and a right cross. He seemed suspended in air for some time. When he landed, it was flat out and very hard, and he moved no more.

Ordinary business was slow in resuming. Bill could not speak and Sid's arm and hand were virtually useless. The last to regain his feet, except Dow, was Carter, who began by crawling feebly on all fours and stated he thought he was bleeding internally and had broken ribs and a pierced lung; he was hard to understand because his dentures had popped out and fallen under the bed. With his teeth in, he got up and regained a professional attitude. He decided Sid had not sustained a fracture of the ulna. Bill could now talk in whispers and apparently his larynx had suffered no permanent damage from Dow's slash or the kick which had caught him on the knee. Aside from sore knuckles, Biff was unmarked and unshaken.

They plucked Dow off the floor and deposited him on the bed. His face, mouth and brow were bloody and he had a swollen eye. Carter revived him and did a clean-up job, revealing a somewhat depressing sight.

"He's a game little guy," Biff said, "but a sucker for combinations. I always wondered about that karate stuff."

"He still has all his teeth," Carter said, "and he can

[149]

move his jaw. I think he may have some concussion, but he's in no danger."

"Yes, he is," Sidney Ellen said. She had retrieved her gun and was shaking with anger. "I'll shoot the son of a bitch if he ever lifts a finger to me again."

Dow Jones's disappearance aroused national, indeed international, interest. To the annoyance of the police, several hours elapsed before his servants and associates turned in an alarm. Evidently they feared he had gone off on some private expedition (he was given to doing things on the spur of the moment) or might have been seduced by admirers, and thought a premature disclosure of his absence could end in unfortunate publicity. When they did conclude he was missing, his trail had grown cold. A gardener remembered seeing him jogging; two housewives—not in Stone Canyon—busy getting children ready for school had observed a car with a pair of people in it wearing the kind of helmets motorcyclists wore; and a woman later established as an alcoholic testified flatly that she had looked out her front door and seen at least five men in black masks forcing Dow into the rear of a moving van. At that time nothing solid had turned up to indicate a kidnapping. Several witnesses mentioned cars on the road unfamiliar to them, but their testimony was so conflicting as to be valueless. Otherwise, a police spokesman emphasized, the department had absolutely no good leads. That Mr. Jones had met with foul play was pure conjecture. He was apparently in excellent health, successful, without enemies or private entanglements that would suggest a forced flight. Rumors in the entertainment world hinted that Dow, though apparently not an acid-head, could be stoned somewhere or sweating out a bad trip; he and the Four Averages were known to have smoked a little grass and swallowed a few uppers and downers.

Newspapers, television and radio followed events closely. One London columnist asked what else could be expected of a nation torn by crime, racial strife and the revolt of the young? The best always had to pay the price—Presidents, senators, clergymen, and now a shining symbol of youth. A teen-age girl left a heart-broken note to her vanished hero, drenched her ragged clothing in expensive lighter fluid, and left her home for a nocturnal immolation on the Sunset Strip. The stuff evaporated en route and she was unable to set herself alight. She was led away by sheriff's deputies and a small riot ensued. The Averages cried during a filmed interview and compared Dow to Buddha and Mohammed Ali; his transfiguration was part of the Aquarian scene, they said. In Boston a mentalist released the information that Dow was in India meditating and would not return until he had blown his mind. A coroner's office report refuted the notion that a body found under the pier at Huntington Beach was Dow's; it was the remains of a skindiver who had failed to surface a month before.

Nearly a week passed. The Dow Jones story was relegated to the back pages of the papers, and cameramen and sound technicians no longer camped outside Dow's Bel Air house, elbowing paths through assemblages of grieving adolescents.

Suddenly Mort Zimbal issued an electrifying statement: Dow Jones had been kidnapped, his captors claimed he was alive and well and living in impenetrable seclusion, and they wanted a huge sum for his return; if their demands were not met within three days, Dow would be murdered. Every resource of city, county, state and federal law enforcement agencies was being employed to find the boy and bring his abductors to justice. J. Edgar Hoover, speaking in Washington, said the Federal Bureau of Investigation was giving the case a high priority, although communists, campus agitators and racial militants need not look for any let-up in the meantime.

"We are willing to risk Dow Jones's life," Mr. Zimbal said in a press conference heavily attended, "because we want to give law and order every opportunity. Dow would want it that way. But we appeal to his kidnappers to spare him, and promise to pay in full if all else fails."

All else failed. *Variety* headlined the matter: HALF A MILL ASKED FOR HARDROCK KID.

Biff's opening conversation with Mort Zimbal was unsatisfactory. He telephoned him at MAC and a snippy secretary declined to bother her boss until the caller had revealed his purpose.

At a public booth outside a closed filling station in Redondo Beach, Brenda waiting by the curb with the engine of the Cadillac running, Biff said: "I can deliver Dow Jones. If you don't put me through in ten seconds, I'm going to hang up."

Zimbal came on in slightly over the period of the ultimatum. "Mr. Zimbal speaking. What can I do for you?"

Something clicked, and Biff assumed his voice was being recorded; he made it rough and blurry. "Listen. Don't talk. I got Dow. You can have him back in one piece for five hundred grand."

"The hell I can!"

"You got three days. After that we clobber him."

"How do we pay? Who are you? How can I be sure you have him?"

"Quit stalling. You're not going to trace this call. Will you pay?"

"I've got to have more facts. Where can I reach you?"

"The code words are 'Thirty Industrials.' You may get a last chance."

"Somebody here is already calling the cops, you rat bastard!" Zimbal shouted.

Hanging up, Biff sped away with Brenda. Sam and Carter awaited them in Snug Harbor, the latter in bed and far from convinced he had not sustained grave internal injuries. Biff's report produced a chill.

"Don't get discouraged," he said. "At these prices you have to negotiate. Did you really think he wouldn't holler for the police?"

He wasn't as confident as he sounded, but he thought Brenda was eyeing him admiringly and had to put up a brave front. On the return trip he had mentioned the stretch pants she was wearing and said how much he liked women with a good build, and she had appeared pleased. Barring the likelihood of his doing time for the rest of his life in a federal pen, he felt he might achieve happiness with her.

"I suppose our next step is to prove we have the little stinker," Sam said; he bitterly resented Dow's escape attempt and attack on the Seniles, and wished it had come during the pickup and he could have killed him. "How?"

"That's no strain," Biff replied. "We have Dow make a tape and play it for Zimbal. Of course it means Carter has to get up and go see his patient. Okay?"

"Okay," Sam said. "Good idea. I have a little self-contained recorder the size of a cigarette box you can use. You're agreeable, Carter?"

Carter grunted assent. "We're sitting on a volcano," he said.

The Thunderbird, proper license plates restored, had been returned to the airport, but a Plymouth was hired next morning at another Los Angeles International rental agency by Biff, who was disguised and carried a suitcase and requested a weekly rate, mentioning that he expected to transact considerable business while in town. The car was nearly new, and he removed the plates beside a hillside vacant lot in Palos Verdes, covered by Brenda and Carter in the Cadillac, putting a temporary sticker on the rear bumper and taping a registration slip to the inside of the windshield. Sour and wordless, Carter got into the Plymouth with his doctor's bag and drove up the coast. His radio was tuned to a news station, and Biff and Brenda were listening as they went to Long Beach to await Carter's return, but nothing in the endless stream of information and advertising touched upon Dow Jones, nor was his name in the newspapers, and they had monitored early television broadcasts in vain. The cops were obviously sitting on the bomb while they had a preliminary look.

Waved through the Colony gate by the guard and addressed as Dr. Morton, Carter stopped at the green house. He had glumly anticipated the presence of Golda, and in a moment she arrived, accompanied by Harvey.

"Hello, Doctor," she said. "I've been talking to Ethel. She says Ernestine is worse—the poor kid had a weak spell and fell down and hurt herself."

"So I understand," Carter said.

"You got a different car today."

"Yes, the other one belonged to the male nurse."

"Brand new, huh? Like the Thunderbird."

Carter moved on. "Yes. Excuse me."

Sidney Ellen let him in. A long-sleeved blouse concealed her black-and-blue forearm and she walked bent somewhat forward.

"That maid . . ." Carter muttered.

"I'm making friends with her," she said. "She's just curious and lonely."

"You hope. How is your arm?"

"Well, I can use it—to put holes in that meistersinger. And I've got a great big bruise on my stomach and can't quite straighten up."

"Shall I examine you?"

"No, thanks. I'll live—long enough to get even."

"Easy, easy," Carter said. "He's too valuable for cheap revenge."

They went upstairs. Dow sat in a chair removing hair from his legs with a depilatory. His long locks had been done by Bill and were now golden and soft and curly and gathered in a pink ribbon; his eyebrows were plucked, not a hint of beard remained on his face, and his lips were bright with lipstick; only diminishing cuts and bruises and part of a shiner detracted from an amazing transformation. Carter stared at him. Bulged alluringly under his peignoir, the dainty transvestite or whatever he was looked inviting.

"Hi," Bill said. His voice was stronger, but he wore an ascot to conceal the marks on his neck. In spite of a limp, cheeriness and an innocent pride were his. "What do you think of him, Dr. Morton?"

"Her," Dow corrected. He put a palm on his hip and smiled dazzlingly. "Peace, brother."

Carter dissembled his revulsion. "Is your jaw bothering you, Ernestine?"

"I can eat and talk, man."

Carter cautiously examined him. "Headaches? Dizziness? Double vision?"

"They're gone."

"You'll do," Carter said.

"I have falsies on him," Bill said. "He has good legs, don't you think? I wish his feet weren't so big. I'm going to paint his toenails."

"Are you all right?" Carter asked, and he and Sid exchanged glances.

"Fine, thanks."

Carter produced Sam's tape recorder from his bag, then gave them a résumé of the situation. Bill's sunny mood continued, but Sid frowned and shook her head. Most affected was Dow, who stopped contemplating his limbs and appeared at once eager and crushed.

"You mean it's not on the air or in the papers?" he demanded. "Man, this is the news the world has been waiting for!"

"The cops are sitting on it," Bill said. "That's natural, Ernie." He turned to Carter. "We allow him to follow things on TV, Doctor."

"How admirable," Carter said, biting off his words.

"Five hundred big ones . . ." Dow said. "All that bread! But you should have asked seven fifty or even a mill. How can any value be set on a property like me?"

"I agree," Carter told him. "Now, you have to make a recording for us—address yourself to Mr. Zimbal—"

"Give me the horn. Listen, I don't dig Mort's attitude. He's escalating this when he ought to be de-escalating." Dow pointed a finger at Sid. "Aunt Ethel is only waiting for a chance to chill me, for God's sake!"

"Yes, yes," Carter said. "Now, be careful what you say. I would suggest—"

"I know what to say." Dow expertly put the tape in motion and held the instrument to his mouth. "Hey, Mort. Mort baby. Your goldmine speaking. Dow Jones. Mort, they got me like put away. I could be put away permanently. You know? There's a crazy old chick ready to bend, staple or mutilate me—like she's waiting for the opportunity. Move it, Mort! You know. You could lose me. Call off the fuzz and pay." He paused. "Listen, nobody could fake this." He sang a few of the many verses of "Big-Butted Baby." "Hey, Mort sweetheart. Mr. Zimbal. I'm waiting. Love and kisses." He reversed the tape and played his appeal. "Here, Doctor. You don't get quality but the voice comes through. This'll make 'em cry. Every kid in America will fall out of his tree."

Carter accepted the recorder, put it away, and retired to the upstairs hall. Bill and Sid followed him, leaving the door open, and Dow went back to his fuzzy calves.

"You have him on the Thorazine?" Carter said quietly to Bill.

"Yes. He's sorry for the fight and gave his word—"

"We can't trust him again. Increase the dosage."

"Listen," Bill said, "I can guarantee his conduct. We've become friends. You won't believe this, but he enjoys being here."

"I don't believe it," Carter said. "Get back in the room and watch him."

Sid accompanied him to the lower floor. "What's going on up there?" he asked.

"Well, Dow seems to like beauty treatments and getting dressed up."

"And Bill?"

"He likes working on him." Sid sighed. "They like each other."

"What about security?"

"Bill carries a blackjack and I always have my gun. At night we handcuff him and tie his ankles. We set the alarm and stand watches of four hours. Dow is usually groggy. A light is always on. The phone upstairs is disconnected and the one down here has a lock on it. All the doors are locked and the windows shut, and downstairs the curtains are closed."

"Humphh. What is Bill going to do if we have to get around to killing Dow?"

"I don't know. It'll be hairy."

"We'll rue the day we ever saw that wailing sexual deviate," Carter said. "Mark my words."

They stepped outside, and, inevitably, Golda was there. Carter informed her that Ernestine was weak but improving and grudgingly thanked her for her interest. Golda replied she was dying to see the kid and to be of help. Hooking arms with her, Sid said she felt sure Golda could pay a visit to her dear niece in the next few days. Seeing no means of protesting such rashness at the moment, Carter got gloomily into the car and drove away. The last he saw of Sid she was petting the dog. And no doubt upstairs, Carter thought, Bill was petting the captive. He was gnawed by the fear that his mob was abandoning discipline and were doomed because of success and overconfidence.

Biff also fell victim to the laxity, perhaps inspired to bravado by a word or two of praise from Brenda. The tape recorder in his pocket, he strolled over to the administrative center, entered a telephone booth, rang MAC, interrupted a woman giving the organization greeting, and said, "Thirty Industrials." In seconds an agitated secretary informed him that a crisis had called Mr. Zimbal to Rome.

Biff said, "I don't need him, and I know you're recording. Take this down." Enfolded in a handkerchief he pretended to hold to his nose was the recorder; he clicked it on, put it to the phone mouthpiece, and delivered Dow's message. Then he hung up and scuttled off.

The promptness of Biff's return from his mission to the strategy conference being held at Carter's house infuriated the doctor. He was further exacerbated by Biff's airy explanation that he was tired of worrying about traced telephone calls.

"Hubris!" Carter said. "You wouldn't know what that means, of course. The hell with all of you. I'm tired of remonstrating."

He sulked, and Biff held the floor and shone in a new limelight. His view prevailed.

"Let's wait," he advised. "Sit tight. The longer we stall, the more nervous Zimbal will get. When he doesn't hear from us, he'll worry about Dow getting knocked off—which means he's got to find out, to come to us some way—which means that sooner or later the cops are bound to tell him to pay and promise to keep clear until Dow's safety is assured. That is standard procedure in kidnappings. We simply stay in the game and wait to improve our hand."

Existence in the Colony was tolerable. Steady tranquilizing and the novelty of being a girl kept Dow Jones tractable. His injuries healed. He readily adjusted to pitching his voice in an upper register along with other feminine traits, enjoyed the meals Sid prepared, spent a good deal of his time before a mirror and discussing beauty aids with Bill, and watched television. At increasingly frequent intervals he would say "Beautiful!" to express his satisfaction. His only depressed moods were when he reflected upon Mr. Zimbal's intransigency.

"You'd think he would've just laid the bread on you without hesitating," he said. "Man, it's *me* that's involved. How does he know you're flower children—you, I mean, not Aunt Ethel—and wouldn't cream me? It would be a loss for the world, not only MAC. You know? I don't dig Mort. Why would he spill to the cops and run the risk of losing me? You know? Oh, I suppose he thought they could find me. Or he freaked. Or he wants a better deal. He always wants a better deal. You know? That must be it. . . ."

When Zimbal released the news of the kidnapping Dow entered a period of ecstasy. Bill had to buy all the newspapers and magazines for him, literally pry him away from the TV set, and supply a transistor radio he could take to bed. He was indefatigable in listening to his name and the scant details of his disappearance, repeated a hundred times, and brooded continually on the sensation he had caused.

"Man, does this groove!" he kept saying. "It's the greatest. What coverage! You think any publicity man could have done it? You know? Like we got a nuclear war, man. Like the sailing of the *Titanic* or the Acropolis."

"Apocalypse," Bill said.

"Yeah, man! It's large."

Dow's euphoria sagged after he learned Zimbal had gone to Rome. "Split?" he cried. "Split? Impossible! With me snatched? How could he? Has he got a bigger deal than me, man?"

Even worse, his message on tape was neither mentioned nor released to an anxious public. He wept, and Bill had to pat his shoulder and renew his makeup. Bill's consoling words on how the police were being crafty and Mr. Zimbal was just playing for time had no effect.

"They're ruining my act," Dow said. "You know? The whole country should be listening to me. It would have killed them." He choked up again. "I'm forgotten. Nobody cares. My own agent blows!" His cheeks reddened under the powder. "I wouldn't mind pounding on that goddam Mort!"

Sidney Ellen grew bored and nervous as the days passed. The forebodings of Carter loomed larger. She hadn't grown to like Dow in the least, and Bill's happy domesticity grated on her. One night she dreamed vividly of J. Edgar Hoover, round and rosy and all smiles, approaching to tap her on the shoulder. She awakened feeling touched by an omen and dampened by chilly perspiration.

Golda was a great trial to her, but unavoidable. They exchanged confidences, walked to the market together, and traded recipes and knitting instructions. Golda said she was extremely lonely now that she was old and didn't make new acquaintances easily, and she missed Miss Gallo. The actress's boyfriend never came home these days. Ethel, she said, was a godsend to her. She pressed continually to see dear little Ernestine, if only for a minute, and Sid knew such a visit, with Golda's bullhorn-spread in the Colony, would help to allay curiosity and suspicion. But she hated taking the risk of something going wrong or Dow making a break.

At length Sid decided it was worth chancing, if merely to shatter the monotony. Carter had counseled against the move, but he wasn't out in the field trying to keep things going and enduring the twitterings of Dow and Bill. The latter had no objections; in fact, he welcomed the test, was proud of his handiwork, and confident he could control Dow. Exhibiting their prisoner tickled his sense of irony. Accordingly, one afternoon he fed his charge an extra dose of pills.

"What a trip!" Dow said. "See if my toes are curled, Uncle Rod."

Arrayed in pink, propped up in bed, blooming from cosmetics, hair curled, long eyelashes fastened to his upper lids, unhandy feet hidden under the covers, Dow awaited the audience. He was dazed but affable, and eager to entertain. Bill held a mirror so he could have a final look at himself.

"Groovy," he commented. "Bring the old cat in and we'll have some girl talk."

Sid said grimly, "Get funny or make a wrong move, Ernestine, and you'll get it. And remember you'll be taking Golda and a poor dog with you."

"Yes, Aunt Ethel," Dow said. "Listen, stop waving that cannon. It might go off."

"He'll be all right," Bill said. "He's a good girl. Aren't you, Ernie?"

"Affirmative, man."

"Keep the voice high and watch your language. Don't forget you're not well."

"Oh, I'm well, Uncle Rod," Dow said. "It's only that I'm so high. Higher than my voice, man."

He received Golda modestly and languidly, spoke of his love for his relatives, patted Harvey, and said his health was improving.

"Why, honey, you're *pretty*," Golda told him. "A girl with your looks has got everything to live for. Except for a few little things, you don't even look as if you'd been sick."

"That's very sweet of you to say," Dow said. "I think I'll be up and around in no time. Won't I, Uncle Rod?"

"Dr. Morton says it is only a matter of time," Bill replied. "All you need is rest."

After a few minutes he decided Ernestine was tiring. Golda made her goodbyes and promised to send over bread pudding, a dish she specialized in.

"Take care of yourself, honey," she said. "You got all your life ahead of you."

"Oh, I hope so," Dow said. "I want so much to have children and a home. Thank you very much for coming, Golda."

"Anything I can do, kid," Golda said, "let me know. Your Aunt Ethel and me are good friends."

Bill smoothed the pillows and gently lowered Dow. He arranged Dow's hair and brought the sheet up to his chin. He patted Dow's hand.

"I'm afraid you've overdone," he said. "Rest, my dear. Have a good nap."

"Uncle Rod," Dow said, "like you've been a mother to me. . . . Give me a kiss."

Bending, Bill pressed his lips to Dow's bedizened cheek and tiptoed to a chair. Sid's stomach churned. She led Golda downstairs.

"Wait'll I tell everybody here how good-looking she is," Golda said. "It breaks your heart to see a kid like that laid out flat on her back. She's got a sweet nature, too."

"Ernestine is a happy child."

"Say, she's got a nice build—so why the padding?"

"Uh, you noticed that?"

"Yeah. I mean the falsies. It don't seem right."

"Well," Sid said, "Ernestine is awfully sensitive about her, uh, lack of development. Rodney and I thought filling her out, so to speak, might be a morale booster."

"To me, Sid, she's too sweet and innocent for that kind of stuff. Just tell her to wait until she's a nursing mother and everything'll hang out all right."

"Perhaps I should."

"One thing that ain't underdeveloped is her feet. I could see them sticking up under the sheet."

"Yes, they're quite large. She's also sensitive about that."

"Another thing I noticed," Golda said, "is how crazy Uncle Rod is about her. Honey, if I was you I'd watch it. Terribly funny things can happen in families."

"Oh, Golda! You shock me!"

"I'm telling you. I've been around. Watch them. It's easy to tell she's got a yen for him, too."

"Golda!"

"You're innocent, honey. Real innocent." Golda shrugged. "And maybe not coming clean with me, huh?"

"I beg your pardon?" Sid looked at Golda with a glacial, unremitting attention, right hand moving toward the automatic under her blouse.

"That ain't just acne on her face. Somebody belted her, right?"

"Wrong. She collapsed, from weakness. We couldn't catch her in time—she hit her head."

"Uh-huh. Come on, she's not that weak."

"I don't like how this conversation is going, Golda. Exactly what are you insinuating?"

"I'll tell you what I'm insinuating: Ernestine's in trouble. She's a tough broad, a delinquent. Maybe she takes drugs—she sure acts like it—and has been busted by the cops. You and Uncle Rod are making the best of it on account of the family, and on account of Uncle Rod is crazy about her. Right?"

"Oh, dear," Sid said.

"She didn't want to stay and straighten out, and you had to cuff her around, huh? Soften her up? Look, I know the signs, and I honor you for it."

"Well, I—"

"You can see she's a hard dame," Golda said. "Plenty of them are these days. Is she pregnant?"

"I—I don't think so."

"Ethel, it isn't easy for you. I know that. But I understand. I'm your friend. A good cuffing is exactly what most of these kids need, but don't go too far and get in the cops."

"I'll try not to."

"Your secret's safe with me. Remember, keep Uncle Rod away from her. She's very sexy."

"Yes," Sid said. "Well—"

"You're making it the hard way, Ethel. I got sympathy for you."

"Thank you." Putting a handkerchief to her eyes, Sid turned aside. "Golda, I can't possibly discuss it now. You'd better leave me alone."

"Sure, kid." Golda patted her shoulder. "Let me know if you want anything. I'm ready to help day or night."

Sid observed Golda's departure through the glass in the rear door, Harvey at her rundown heels. She was wracked by alarm and indecision. Golda was not especially bright, but terribly observant and a rapid theorizer. Sooner rather than later she would accumulate fresh material and arrive at more conclusions. It was a race with time. Their moving next door to her was sheer bad luck, the odd and malefic chance.

Sid's choler rose irrationally. Old Golda merited a bullet, and the prospect of shooting her was growing inviting.

When she told Bill of Golda's revelations, he blanched and said, "This can't go on. I'll plan it for you, if you want."

"Plan what?"

"I'm not sure; I'll give it thought. Maybe she should be seen in a bathing suit—and go swimming with a weight tied to her feet and not come back. We have a nice handy ocean."

"Oh?"

"But you'd have to do it. You're the killer."

"I know," Sid said, and felt a touch of pride.

"Bless me!" Carter said.

He was sitting in Sam's living room watching the color television set. Mr. Zimbal, a small, thin-haired, puffy man in a dark suit and modish collar and wide, flowered tie had just appeared in melting shades of blue, green, red and shabby brown slightly out of focus as usual to offer terms to the abductors of Dow Jones.

"I have returned to the U.S. specifically to assure you," he said, "that your wishes will be met. I pray that you have not gone through with your cruel threat to kill Dow Jones. We are ready to pay, and the lawmen have agreed not to interfere. You can pick up the ransom unhindered. I beg you to get in touch with me, day or night, at my office or home; the call will not be traced—I give you my word on that. Please restore Dow Jones to the world and his millions of fans!"

Mr. Zimbal had been a striking and tragic figure in spite of close-set, hard eyes and the autocratic precision of a wheeler-dealer.

Now a solemn-faced newscaster was playing the tape Dow recorded. It sounded tinny and remote, but authentic. "This is one of the most dramatic moments of history," the newscaster said, at the tape's conclusion. "Through the medium of the all-seeing electronic eye, you have been brought into the very midst of a great crime. Think what the Lindbergh kidnapping could have been with the addition of television cameras!"

"What's the matter, Carter?" Sam asked.

"We're so dumb and careless. None of us caught the part where the little pervert mentioned an old woman waiting to kill him. That should have been eliminated."

"Why?"

"Because it helps to identify us, damn it! To furnish another gratuitous hazard. It's bound to bring up that 'Grandma Bandit' stuff again."

"Oh, now, Doctor," Biff chided. "That's really reaching."

"I know matters have reached a dangerous point," Carter retorted, "when you exhibit bravery and confidence."

Arising, Sam shut off the TV. "Biff, what's the next step?"

Biff smiled at Brenda and cleared his throat importantly. "Maybe what gave me confidence was flattening Jones. If I hadn't been right there—"

"Yes, yes," Sam said. "Stick to the subject."

"Well, we got them by the short hairs. It needn't be complicated. I negotiate, we cash our check, and Sid takes care of Dow."

"No you don't," Brenda said. "No, sir!"

"Yes we do," Sam said. "I'm not buying any sentimentality. We can't leave key witnesses—and that includes that damn maid who has been worrying Sid."

"Wait a minute," Carter said. "You're all such egregious fools. You are probably not going to dare kill anybody, and you certainly are not going to be able to simply cash a check. Don't you understand conditions are nothing like what we anticipated? Have you no conception of the man you're dealing with?"

"How's it changed?" Biff said.

"I didn't expect you to notice." Carter shifted to Sam. "Look here, Major. You're a man with brains. You must know Zimbal is as tough and crafty as he looks. What did he do when Biff first talked to him? He told Biff where to get off and called the police. And he went away in the middle of the commotion to transact business in Europe. Zimbal doesn't really give a hoot for Dow—he could get some other degenerate to replace him day after tomorrow if we killed him—he's been forced into this gesture of surrender because of public opinion and the publicity value accruing to him and Dow. The failure of the cops and FBI to find Dow, and Zimbal's basic assumption that it would be too costly for us to murder him out of hand, has forced Zimbal into another option. It's a pure matter of dollars and cents with him."

"But you said yourself Dow should write the check," Biff interposed. "That was one of the reasons we got into it—"

"Shut up," Sam rasped. "Yes, Carter?"

"When we dealt with the insurance company," Carter continued. "we were handling minor crooks. Zimbal is a *big* crook. He is going to pay only as much for

Dow as his value warrants, and if we'd had sense enough to think things out correctly beforehand instead of listening to Bill's siren song we would have realized payment by check was impossible. As ordinary thieves outwitted by other thieves, it was to the insurance company's advantage to keep the transacion quiet and not pursue an investigation. But Zimbal is a different kind of operator, and we have perpetrated a major crime known throughout the world. Do you seriously believe he wouldn't pursue this afterwards in Switzerland, with the help of the U.S. government? Under certain conditions, when criminality is suspected, Swiss banks will break the secrecy of numbered accounts. We could be tracked down inside of a week. Zimbal has influence. Probably he has accounts like mine. He knows the ropes."

"Uh-huh. I see."

"Furthermore, you can't kill Dow. It isn't that easy. You'll have to be as bright as Zimbal if you hope to collect. Nothing is more naïve than to assume he'd pay a penny—and most of the ransom, I suspect, will have to come from whatever Dow has left after taxes—without having him in his hands and in good condition. Either take thought or forget your dreams of wealth."

"Ummm," Sam said. "Yes." He and Carter were starting to observe an odd, incisive formality. "Doctor, we've got to have a serious private talk."

"Carty—" Brenda said.

"Biff will take you to a movie," Carter said.

"Me?" Biff said. "Am I in on this or not?"

"I don't want to go with him," Brenda said. She regarded her husband admiringly. "Carty, you're wonderful!"

"Oh, my ass!" Carter said impatiently.

"That's a funny way for a doctor like you to talk," Brenda said, and smiled.

Thoroughly coached and almost wholly deflated, Biff went for a long drive alone and telephoned MAC from a pay station in San Bernardino. Sun blazed on the glass enclosure and he was sweaty and irritable.

"Thirty Industrials," he said to the operator.

The corporation switchboard chattered.

"All right," Mort Zimbal said. "Go ahead."

"He's alive."

"I know that. What else?"

"I don't hear the recording sound. You better put this down. You may need to refer to it, because you're only going to hear it once."

"I'll remember."

"How do you know he's alive?"

"You're not dealing with a sucker. Unless I see him unharmed before I pay, you don't get a penny."

"Impossible. You have to take my word—"

"Then forget it."

Biff collected his thoughts; Zimbal had a convincing manner. "Well, that might be arranged. Now about the ransom—"

"The first figure you quoted is ridiculous."

"We won't take less, Mr. Zimbal."

"Then get off the line. I'm busy."

"Listen, you got to have him."

"Have I? Try me."

There was a brief silence, and Zimbal added, "I'm hanging up."

"I'm thinking!" Biff said. "Who's in the driver's seat, you or me?"

"Me. I'm willing to pay a good price. Dow can't. He's absolutely worthless to you unless you come to terms with me. I am ready to offer you an open end deal."

"Huh?"

"We ran this through the computer—Dow's future earnings, popularity expectancy, the publicity factor you introduced, what he's worth to us. He has eighty thousand in liquid assets, and we'll add two hundred thousand. That's tops."

"Now wait a minute—"

"You haven't heard the rest of the deal, dummy," Zimbal said cuttingly. "If you're afraid and can't deliver him, we will pay you fifty thousand by mail or messenger, secrecy guaranteed, as soon as we have authentication of Dow's death. My reason is that I think you are a bunch of amateurs and might simply release him in a moment of panic. I don't want Dow back and being a nuisance once we have written him off."

Gulping, Biff said, "We're not a bunch of amateurs. Oh, maybe compared to you—"

"Correct. But wait till I'm through giving you the deal, will you? We're going to say we have paid five hundred thousand for Dow and claim it as a business loss. Our lawyer believes we can, although this may involve some litigation with the government. Therefore I don't want you caught and the true amount of the payment disclosed."

"Oh."

"We will draw five hundred thousand-dollar bills for the ransom, after collecting the eighty thousand from Dow's account, over which we exercise power of attorney. Two hundred eighty bills will go to you. The other two hundred twenty bills will be deposited in our private fund. Through an oversight, the piece of paper containing the numbers of the bills can be lost in the excitement. Your protection is our protection. We stand to make a profit, and your payment and safety are assured. A half-million-dollar ransom makes Dow seem more important and increases the publicity spread."

Biff was blinking, "Ah . . ."

"Which end of the deal you want?"

"Mr. Zimbal, you couldn't go a little higher? I have to get back to my associates—"

"No. dummy."

"Being rude doesn't help any, Mr. Zimbal," Biff said. "Well, I'll take this up with—"

"You have exactly twenty-four hours," Zimbal interrupted. "As of four o'clock tomorrow afternoon we are closing out Dow unless we hear from you."

"Now just a minute there—" The click of a disconnected line rang in Biff's ear.

He went back to Snug Harbor a trifle dazed, and the council convened. His description of the conversation produced profound astonishment in everybody but Carter.

"And we think we're bright and crooked," Sam said. "Move over, chumps."

"Why, what a terrible person!" Brenda said. "He must have ice water in his veins."

"Antifreeze," Biff replied. "Mixed with snake venom." He feared he was losing importance in her eyes. "Don't get the idea we didn't have a hell of an argument. I would not take anything from him. I really worked on this deal. It's the best I can do—"

"The best Zimbal can do," Carter said. He pressed in his slipping teeth and rubbed his jaws reflectively. "One must admire him, however. Compared to him, we *are* amateurs. But the question is, can we trust him? His offer could be part of an elaborate plan for snaring us when we deliver the little catamite."

"We got an open end, thanks to me," Biff said. "There's fifty thousand just for knocking off the kid. We could have the money delivered to a third party in an unmarked package, and wait a while—"

"Shame on you!" Brenda said. "If you touch the poor guy I'll go to the cops myself."

"I have a feeling Bill would beat you to it," Carter told her. "No, that's out . . ." He straightened, snapping his fingers, virtually smiling. "Speaking of Bill gives me an idea. Possibly we can deliver Dow with a minimum of risk."

"Carty," Brenda said, "you're the greatest."

"Without the deal I got him," Biff said, "where would he be?"

"Shut up," Sam said. "You were saying, Doctor?"

From the Long Beach airport early next morning Biff took a plane to San Diego, and used a public telephone to call MAC. "Thirty Industrials" brought prompt action.

"Yes?" Mort Zimbal said.

"We accept."

"What?"

"You get Dow. Have you the money?"

"I'll get it. When is delivery?"

"Any time in the next forty-eight hours. Give me an idea of where we can contact you."

"I'm usually here in the office from ten o'clock in the morning until seven or eight o'clock in the evening, except for lunch." Zimbal gave Biff his Beverly Hills home address and private telephone number. "Most nights I am out to dinner or in a studio seeing movies, but the switchboard can always reach me. Understand this: I am not going to meet you in some abandoned rock quarry or up in the mountains where you can put a bullet into me, and I will have a man with me at night who is armed. Anyway, even though the police and federal men have promised to keep hands off until Dow is freed, they're no doubt keeping an eye on me—which means I can't take any long trip."

"Okay," Biff said. "We might drop in on you at your house kind of late."

"Don't do that. I think police are staked out. Call me and I'll arrange to go to the house of a friend."

"Yes, Mr. Zimbal. Put the money in a briefcase and keep it with you all the time. I mean *all* the time."

"Don't try to impress me. The bills will remain locked in my office or home safe until I have seen Dow. I'm calling the shots, dummy."

"Right, Mr. Zimbal. Goodbye."

Dropping more quarters into the coin box, Biff then telephoned Sam at Sunset Town. "Deal closed," he said.

Warned by an advance call from Brenda impersonating Dr. Morton's nurse, Sidney Ellen sent a pleased Bill off on an errand to a boutique on Pacific Coast Highway. To ensure that nothing went wrong in Bill's absence, she had him shackle Dow to the bed and then sat down to keep guard with fingers clasped around the butt of the gun beneath her apron. The precautions somewhat dampened Dow's high spirits.

"Why so uptight, Grandma?" he asked. "What's happening?"

"Call me 'Grandma' again and you'll wish you hadn't."

As Carter had anticipated, in the prodigious flap that followed Mr. Zimbal's dramatic appeal to Dow Jones's kidnappers, the informational media had not failed to note mention of the crazy old chick just hoping to bend, staple or mutilate him and had promptly revived the legend of the "Grandma Bandit." This development enchanted Dow, who was luxuriating in the mad outpouring about him. "Beautiful, beautiful," he said at intervals. "Now I rank with the moon men. You know? It couldn't get bigger. They'll pay half a mill! Hey, wasn't Mort great on the tube? I thought he was going to cry. Like everybody's waiting for me—*everybody*. You know? I'll never be forgotten. I'll be the biggest property in show biz. You know?"

Now he pouted. He hardly touched the early lunch Sid served him on a tray.

"I had breakfast a little while ago," he complained. "I'm not hungry."

"Eat it. You'll need your strength."

"Why? Are we going to split?"

She hesitated. "Pretty soon."

"Today?"

"Perhaps."

"Naw," he said. "Let it build. Give 'em the old suspense. You know? Keep 'em crying for more."

"Knock it off and eat, Ernestine."

He traded glares with her. "Yes, Grandma."

The atmosphere was tense when Bill returned laden with packages. He glanced from one to the other of them and sighed.

"Ethel," he said, "I've asked you not to be too hard on Ernie. He's cooperating."

"Hey, Uncle Rod," Dow said. "I'm all right. You know? I like the pad. I kept my promise about no more rumbles. I did an act for the old cat next door. Right? But Grandma is rude to me."

"Go ahead," Sid said. "Keep on calling me 'Grandma.'"

"Girls, girls . . ." Bill said.

Opening the purchases calmed Dow. He was gladdened by the bell-bottom floppy pants, loose blouse and fringed leather jacket intended for him, although he said a dress would have pleased him better; a short dress, kind of mod and mini, because he thought his legs were maybe his best feature.

"Oh, no," Bill said. "I see you as more hippie and farther out, Ernie. You'll be darling this way. I'll change your makeup to *crazy*."

"Well, maybe. You think so?"

"Of course. Pull your jockstrap up in those tight pants, please. We don't want any queer bulges, do we?"

"No. Hey, Uncle Rod—do we have to bomb out today? It's cool here. I'm happy. You know? Full of Doc Morton's joy juice all the time. I've never been stoned so good. What's the hurry?"

Bill's face tightened. "Has Aunt Ethel told you?"

"Yeah."

"Ernie, I've been dreading this moment. . . . No, it can't be put off. We must part. That's the way it goes. . . ."

Tears sprang in Dow's eyes. He refused to continue being fitted with a pair of flat-heeled slippers Bill had managed to find. He bowed his head. Bill's arm went around him, and they clung together desolately.

"I never had any home life," Dow said slowly. "My parents separated and both got married again. They didn't want me. I was always uptight. You know? You've changed it, Uncle Rod. You know?"

Stifled, Sid fled downstairs. Somehow Dow's sincere sorrow and Bill's frustrated affection had affected her. The odd thing, she perceived, was that they had established a sort of household here, almost a refuge—two old folks harboring a wayward girl. She shook her head irritably as she prepared sandwiches. On the eve of the great test, her mind was going. . . .

The door buzzer sounded. She unlocked the back door to admit Carter, catching a glimpse of the omnipresent Golda and Harvey.

"Yes, she's out there," he said fretfully. "Damn her! She intimated to me that she knows Jones is pregnant and takes dope!"

"Yes, she has numerous ideas. I thought it best not to deny anything as long as she wasn't on the right track. And if we can get away all right, it doesn't matter."

"Oh, but it does. She has observed Bill buying women's clothing and suspects something is in the wind. But that isn't the worst. She has attached herself to you and can furnish an exact description, and she'll do no less with Bill."

"Do you think I ought to finish her off?" Sid asked.

Carter groaned. "I don't know. I suppose you should, but I hate to issue an order. I'll leave it up to you. However, I feel it's fair to say to you that lack of guts on your part may put us all in jeopardy."

"Okay."

"If you do act, also make sure of the dog—he mustn't be free to attract attention."

"Yes. Okay."

"What is going on upstairs? Is Ernestine tractable?"

"The last I saw of him, he was crying. He and Uncle Rod are pretty broken up at having to part."

"Good God! Has Uncle Rod fallen for him? Can it cause us trouble?"

"No," Sid said. "I don't think they have a real affair —Uncle Rod is too old and he still limps. But he has been a mother to the punk. I'd say they were romantic and maternal."

Carter scowled. "Have Uncle come down here. I must brief you."

"Besides," Sid added, "the relationship, such as it is, has been a help to us. Ernestine has been easier to handle." She remembered a word she had picked up from Dow. "Carter, remember this is Uncle's bag. He's got us where we are."

"Indeed he has!"

"Well, please don't pick on him."

She ascended the stairs. A calmer Dow was standing in front of a closet door mirror, his slippers on, having his hair arranged in long, clotted folds by Bill, who had a spray can and a comb.

"It'll be groovy with you in drag too," Dow said. "Man, this is wild! You know? I can't wait to see Mort at the confrontation! What a dialogue! Meaningful, man!"

"You won't recognize me," Bill said. "I'm going as a *matron*."

"Mother!" Dow said, and beamed.

"Lock him up, Uncle Rod," Sid ordered. "Come below for a conference. Dr. Morton wants us."

Dow protested whiningly at being handcuffed and tied. He glared at Sid.

"Listen, Grandma," he said. "I got my thing and you got your thing, and never the twain will meet. You know? You burn my butt. Who's important here, you or I? Who are they giving the bread for? Who are you making a fortune off of?"

"Off, you tippy-toed illiterate," Sid snarled.

"Yeah?" Dow said. "Just wait, Grandma. Who am I going to finger when I'm loose? You, and nobody else. Not Uncle Rod or that old doctor, but just you. Just you, Grandma. You know?"

"Go on," Sid said. "Keep asking for it and you'll get it."

"Please!" Bill cried. "You're driving me out of my *mind!"*

"I'm sorry, Uncle Rod," Dow said.

Pale and distracted, Bill blinked back the moisture in his eyes and followed Sid down the staircase. Carter launched immediately into his instructions. Bill stood, chin drooping, without comment.

"This is very complicated," Carter said, in summing up, "and the timing must be precise. We are acting quickly in order to achieve an element of surprise. Under such conditions, something could easily go wrong—in fact, unquestionably will—and you've got to keep alert." He paused, and addressed himself to Bill. "You seem depressed, Uncle Rodney. Why? Are you afraid? Haven't we arrived at the culmination of what you suggested? Do you have any objections?"

"No," Bill said. He lifted pained eyes to Carter. "Only I wish I'd never got into it."

"Ah? I hope we can count on you to do your part."

"I won't fail you. . . . The main thing is we're not killing him. I would never have agreed to that."

"You would damn well have agreed to what the rest of us decided," Carter snapped. "We are a criminal gang, not a lonely hearts club." He distributed capsules. "These are for you—particularly Uncle Rodney. And here is Ernestine's dosage, to be taken approximately half an hour before you leave." He walked to the door, motioning for Sid to come along. "Good luck. Take care. I trust we will gather tonight for a celebration."

Speechless, Bill wheeled blindly away and slowly climbed the stairs, taking a careful step at a time like the old man he suddenly was. Watching him go, Carter pursed his lips.

"You've got to take charge, Sid," he said. "That idiot has lost his head."

"Okay."

"Showing the least weakness now is a sure means of ruining us."

"Yes."

Carter started through the doorway, turned back, and thrust out his hand. "Good luck. You are the best among us. I know I can count on you."

"Thanks, Carter," she said. "I admire you. If we don't meet again, or meet in the wrong place . . . well, you know what I mean."

Stiff-faced, they marched out. Golda and Harvey awaited them.

"You must follow my instructions exactly, Miss Smith," Carter said, for Golda's benefit.

"Yes, Doctor."

"How is she, Doctor?" Golda asked.

"I am not satisfied with Miss Potts's condition. Miss Smith and her brother are going to bring her to the hospital for tests."

"No kidding? You're sure it's the hospital?"

"I beg your pardon?" Carter said.

Golda grinned. "Just a little gag, Doctor. Don't give it a thought."

Staring at her as he got in the car, Carter summoned Sid to him with a waggled forefinger. "A confidential word with you, Miss Smith." Their heads came together. "That settles it," he whispered. "Dispose of her."

"Yes, Dr. Morton," Sid said. "Goodbye."

She stood watching Carter drive off, Golda beside her and evincing some signs of excitement.

"Ethel," she said, "this kind of upsets me. I guess I won't be seeing Ernestine again, huh?"

"Of course you will. It's only that the doctor wants to put her under observation. Now, why would you say anything like that?"

"Oh, I don't know." Golda laughed knowingly. "I don't always need the building to fall in on me, honey."

Growing colder, muscles tightening, Sid said: "What are you talking about, Golda?"

"Nothing. Forget it. . . . Can I say so long to Ernestine?"

Sidney Ellen hesitated, agonizing over the degree of Golda's knowledge and the latitude she could be allowed. Obviously she knew too much, perhaps fatally too much. But grabbing her right now was risky—they were in the open, people were distantly in view, others were on the beach, a car could pass; Golda might resist or scream, or Harvey be impossible to handle outside. She had no choice but to wait.

"By all means," she said. "Ernestine will be heartbroken if she doesn't see you. Come by in half an hour when we have her ready for the trip. Be sure to bring Harvey, because Ernestine adores him."

"Thanks," Golda said. "I sure wouldn't want to miss *this*."

Sid went back inside. She glared through the glass of the door at Golda's retreating back, wanting to put a bullet through it. Sweat gathered on her upper lip and she absently brushed off the drops. She walked into the living room, struggling to subdue her panic; Golda might already be telephoning an alarm, or be on her way to the gate to inform the guard. Bill appeared at the head of the stairs, clasping and unclasping his hands.

"He's crying," he said. "I can't stand it. He's gone all to pieces. Can't I give him one of the pills now?"

"Give 'em to yourself," Sid replied grimly. "Golda

knows something. She said so. If she doesn't come back here in half an hour to see Ernestine, we're done for. I've got to kill her. . . ."

"I don't care," Bill said. "Everything's washed up for me."

At Snug Harbor the main body of Seniles assembled in Carter's house and rehearsed movements and emergency procedures and gathered equipment. Biff received Sam's service automatic, and Sam himself concealed the machine pistol underneath his clothing, suspended by a strap. Looking tense and testy, Carter ordered them out. To avoid inviting the curiosity of neighbors, Sam and Biff left first in Biff's car carrying the odds and ends they would require suitably camouflaged in packages and cartons. After an interval the Tildens followed, Carter moving stiffly to emphasize the condition of his arthritis; they waved and spoke to the couple across the street, who toiled on their front patch of dichondra, mentioning that they were going to the club. Brenda drove the Cadillac.

"It's getting to seem like old stuff now, isn't it?" she remarked.

Carter grunted and looked straight ahead. He was fearful and uncertain, and despised himself for being relieved that neither he nor his wife would really be on the firing line of this one.

A considerable distance beyond Golden Years, they stopped on the side street where Sam had parked and locked his car and picked up him and Biff and their impedimenta. Snuggled down on the rear floor of the Cadillac, Sam and Biff removed outer clothing and slipped into the coveralls that had served them in the bank job and now had ACME BUILDING MAINTENANCE CO in stenciled block letters on the backs, sewn on by Brenda. She put on a floppy hat and dark glasses, tied a scarf around her neck, and added a shapeless sweater. Then she removed makeup and helped Carter to affix abundant white hair and a stiff, small white moustache and prescription sunglasses. Biff added a brown wig and a moustache to his ensemble, but Sam disdained to change his appearance. He was mean, silent and gimlet-eyed.

"It's strange," Biff said chattily. "I always feel like going to the bathroom the minute we start."

"Crap in your coveralls," Sam said. "There's plenty of room."

"Major Crawford!" Brenda said.

"I beg your pardon," Sam said.

"If we are going to allow robbery and kidnapping to make vulgarians of us," Brenda said, "I for one say we'd better stop right—"

"Oh, for God's sake!" Carter said. *"Shut up!"*

Pouty and flushed, Brenda drove swiftly on the freeway. Conversation was ended. In Inglewood she stopped two blocks away from the truck rental agency in which she had earlier initiated proceedings for renting a half-ton pickup, and she and Carter walked the remainder of the distance. Brenda had explained that they were moving from a little house to an apartment in the San Fernando Valley and couldn't afford the cost of a moving van, and the man in the office was kind and helpful.

"I brought my husband to help me run the truck," she said.

In truth, operating it was nearly beyond Carter's capabilities, which constituted the main reason for Brenda's presence. He used a false name and driving license in signing up. Brenda had told the man they were pensioners and very short of money, and although he exacted a deposit in cash, he assured them a night man would be on at the agency and they could get a reduction in fee by returning the rig as soon as they were moved.

"But listen," he counseled, "don't you folks overdo. Take it easy. Even with Medicare it's no fun to spend a week or two in bed just because you tried to save a few bucks."

Carter tottered realistically, and they promised to be careful and then departed. A fast exchange of personnel and equipment was negotiated as soon as they rejoined Biff and Sam, who drove off in the pickup. Resuming at the wheel of the Cadillac, Brenda took her husband to Santa Monica, where he had spotted the Plymouth in a public garage, and dropped him off. He removed the temporary sticker from the bumper and the registration document from the windshield, and gave an attendant money for putting on what he said were his new license plates. Thereafter he went to Los Angeles International, returned the car and paid for it in cash, and entered a lounge to await a commuter flight to Long Beach.

Sidney Ellen kept an eye on the clock as she worked. She had telephoned Golda, more to reassure herself than anything else, and delayed their meeting for an additional half hour. Golda had made no further comment and sounded reasonably calm. Notwithstanding, Sid perspired. The uncertainty was maddening, the prospect of having to do Golda in was nothing like pleasurable. Dr. Tilden's chemical restoratives palliated the worst of her tension, but she observed her hands trembling.

Bill's attitude was scarcely helpful. His sorrow had been succeeded by fear. Haggard and colorless, he berated Sid in whispers for not getting Golda at once— he felt allowing her any liberty after what she had intimated was madness.

"You've betrayed us," he said. "You lost your nerve."

Red sparks floated through Sid's field of vision. "One more word, you little crumb," she hissed, "and I'll leave you here with that goddam maid!"

He shrank from her, growing even paler. But it was a dubious triumph. She was growing even shakier. She had indeed lost her nerve.

[181]

What she had to do before they departed was almost a relief. It was like, she thought, those old war movies where they closed the embassy, burned the papers, shredded the code books and smashed the secret radio. She gathered all extra clothing and most of their toilet articles and other oddments and crammed them into a suitcase which would accompany Ernestine on her fictitious journey to the hospital. Literally everything had to be wiped to obliterate fingerprints. Various bits and pieces that were flammable went up in the fireplace. Catching sight of her countenance in a mirror, Sid was startled; it was as stony and unrelenting as Sam's at his worst. She smiled in a forced fashion at herself and determined to be more charming once she had murdered Golda.

At her call, Bill brought Dow to the head of the stairs; they descended the steps hand in hand. Tucked under Bill's arm in a paper sack was his female costume, and his free hand held a small makeup case. Dow, as seductive as most modern girls in his ugly clothing, wobbled a little—he was under the influence again and his truculence toward Sid had vanished. He grinned at her vaguely and thrust out his false superstructure.

"Hi, Aunt Ethel," he said. "Like goodbye. You know?"

"Like goodbye," she replied disgustedly. "But first you have to say goodbye to Golda. Sit down. Act weak."

"I don't have to act, Auntie. I'm on another trip."

"Golda's going on a trip too."

"Please," Bill said. "I'm *upset,* Ethel."

"Why are you always putting me down?" Dow asked. "You're always on a bummer. What's your hang-up, Aunt Ethel?"

"Shut up."

"See? I've never met a dame who can keep her warm as long as you. You're rude. All that bread they're laying on you for me means nothing."

"It means something," Bill said. He glanced at Sid and could not repress a shudder. "That's why she hasn't killed you, Ernie. Believe me!"

"Oh," Dow said. "Yeah, man. I believe you." He gazed at Sid wide-eyed. "Look at that kisser!"

She tried to change expression, to soften what she supposed were Grant Wood lines. It was hard. Golda was two minutes late. Sid's mouth was dry, her eyes burning, the palms of her hands wet. Footsteps outside in the rear congealed her and Bill. They could belong to cops coming to get them. She took out her gun, and Bill gripped his in his pocket.

"There's that cannon again. . . ." Dow said.

"Hi," Golda called. "Ethel? Here I am."

Sid cocked her head at Bill, who stepped aside, out of range of the door. She held the automatic behind her back and unlocked and opened the door, straining to see beyond Golda, breath stopped, half expecting blue uniforms and the glint of weapons. Golda was apparently alone except for the dog, but that was not greatly reassuring. Sid admitted her, closed and locked the door, and turned stiffly, the gun still concealed.

Regarding her affably, Golda said, "You look kind of jumpy, honey. I'm not surprised." She looked at Bill, moving warily from his ambush. "Hi, Uncle Rod. Nervous?"

"No," Bill said, in a squeaky voice. "Hello."

"It makes me sad to have you go," Golda said. "I'm going to be real lonesome without you."

"Why, we're just taking Ernie to the hospital," Bill began, "and then we'll—"

"Never mind," Sid said.

Golda dominated the scene. She went up to the chair where Dow was slumped, saying, "And here's the poor little sick girl looking prettier than ever. Hi, Ernestine."

Dow pushed his bright tresses aside and gazed at her blinkingly. "Hi, Aunt Golda—I mean Golda. Nice of you to drop by. I got to go to the hospital."

"Yeah. The hospital."

"Uh, I'm kind of weak."

"Kind of stoned, don't you mean?"

"How did you know, Aunt Golda?"

"I'm real good at mysteries, Ernestine. Can I give you a goodbye kiss?"

"Yes, sweetie," Dow said graciously.

Bending down, Golda kissed Dow. As she straightened, her head bumped on Sid's pistol.

"The joke's over, Golda," Sid said. "What do you know? Who have you told? Better answer quickly and simply—you haven't got long."

Sid was terribly disconcerted at how Golda looked at her in transparent admiration and affection, her lips parted in a half smile. "Everything, honey. The gun does it. And I haven't told nobody. I'm no informer."

"There's no one outside?" Sid groped for the proper words. "On your honor?"

"I swear it!"

Sid's heart pained ominously. "We have to chance it," she said. "Get him—her out, Uncle Rodney."

Faded in hue and clumsy, Bill struggled with Dow and said, "Come on, Ernie. Come on. Upsy-daisy . . ." He moved forward, supporting his wobbly burden.

"Stand still," Sid said to Golda. "I mean still."

"Yes, Grandma," Golda said worshipfully.

Dow lurched over to pat Harvey's head and was rewarded with a wagging tail. "Ciao, Harv," he said. "You dog." He giggled. "A police dog. You know?"

They reached the door, and Sid unlocked and opened it; she could see nothing untoward in a preliminary sweep. Bill gazed outside in unadulterated dread.

"I'm having the vapors . . . ," he whispered.

"You haven't got time for them. Keep your hand on your gun. If anything happens, fall back here. I'll cover you."

Waving flappily backward during his stumbling descent of the steps, Dow called, "Goodbye, you cats. It's been beautiful. Groovy. You know."

It seemed to Sid that Bill took an hour to half carry, half drag Dow to the garage. She was horrified to note that Bill partially crouched behind the captive, as if to use him as a shield against the world. He had forgotten to keep hold of his gun and was employing both hands on Dow. At last they entered the rear garage door. It closed on them, and Sid shut the kitchen door and sagged against the jamb, gulping air.

"I told you there was nobody," Golda said.

Sid reopened the kitchen door with a shaky grasp. Her ears were straining for the creak of the garage door, which would follow Bill's settling of Dow in the car. She heard the sound of the raising, and nothing followed. After waiting, she again closed the kitchen door and turned to Golda.

"How did you find out?" she demanded.

"Listen, it come to me in a flash—when they started talking about the 'Grandma Bandit' on TV. I knew it was you! And the next thing I had to know was Ernestine was Dow Jones. His feet, the falsies, that hair. And you let me kiss him—you can't see his beard, but you can feel it with your lips. But I was sure before now anyway. Pretty good, huh?"

"Not for you."

"Grandma, I want to join the gang!"

"Stop calling me Grandma, you old bag!"

"I beg your pardon, Ethel," Golda said respectfully. "But I do."

Sid looked at her, eyes filming. "Golda, I hate to do this to you . . ."

"Do what, Ethel?"

"Well—"

"Listen," Golda said, "I admire the hell out of you. You've been nice to me. I wouldn't squeal!" She had realized Sid's purpose and fear seized her and she spoke fast and unsteadily. "You wouldn't do anything to

[185]

a friend, would you? What've I ever done to you? Listen, Ethel—listen, please—I could've told the cops, couldn't I? I didn't! I won't ever say a word! I give you my word! Honest to God! You wouldn't hurt me and Harvey, would you?"

Sid shifted her attention to Harvey, and he thumped his tail on the floor and got up to come over and lick the fingers of the hand she instinctively extended to him. His opaque green eyes glowed with love and trust. Whatever Golda might be, *he* was the most candid, innocent and decent of creatures. Sighing, Sid grew aware she was not going to harm Harvey. Besides that, she'd be damned if she'd shoot his best friend either. Any friend of Harvey's was a friend of hers.

"Jesus H. Christ!" Golda said. "Ethel, honey, I'll forget everything I—"

"Never mind," Sid said. "But shut up and come with me."

She opened the suitcase and got the handcuffs, wide surgical tape and gauze. The three of them went into the maid's bathroom, adjoining the kitchen. Upon instruction the pale Golda sat down, partially under the washbasin. Sid handcuffed her to the plumbing. Harvey was amused by the proceedings and frisked around. Then Sid prepared tape and bandages for Golda's eyes and mouth.

"Sorry," she said.

"I understand," Golda replied. "You got a hot situation here, Grandma."

"I don't like that name!"

"Excuse me."

Sid sealed her eyes and mouth, avoiding as far as possible fastening the tape onto hair. She gave Golda a consolatory pat, and held Harvey's muzzle in her hands for a few seconds and implanted a kiss on his low forehead. She closed and locked the window and shut the door on the prisoners. Her last acts were to cut the telephone wires and lock all doors.

Bill was with Dow in the rear seat of the Chevrolet, and Dow seemed pretty far gone. Settling at the wheel, Sid glanced in the rear vision mirror and saw Bill staring at her with very wide eyes set in a colorless face. She started the engine.

"Uh, did you handle it, luv?" he asked.

"Yes."

"She—didn't suffer, did she?"

"They never do," Sid said.

An elderly guard at the gate stopped them, and Sid reached under the folds of her skirt for the pistol. The guard's expression was grave.

"Golda let us know your niece is worse," he said. "We're all real sorry to hear it." He leaned in Sid's window toward Dow. "Don't get discouraged, Miss Potts."

Dow looked at him blankly and belched.

"She's awfully weak," Bill said.

"Well, lots of luck," the guard said.

Driving off, Sid mumbled, "That's what we need, all right."

She sped into an open space across the highway devoted to fields of flowers, and Bill scrambled about on the floor of the rear of the car getting into a wig, blouse, a P.T.A. sort of dressmaker's suit, hose and sensible pumps, and then made himself up. While he was busy, Sid exchanged gray hair for blond, wriggled into a black dress and white sweater, discarded her spectacles and put in her contact lenses, and applied more youthful cosmetics. Dow, watching them dreamily, suddenly slid downward. Bill had to prop him up.

"Carter's overdone it this time," he complained. "He's on the ropes. What do we do if he can't stand up?"

"Kill ourselves," Sid said. "I'm looking forward to it."

In Santa Monica, half an hour later, Brenda was waiting two spaces up from the parking place Sid backed into. Bill had spent the intervening minutes rubbing Dow's hands, fanning him, exhorting until he was hoarse. Miraculously, his charge revived, said, "Beautiful!" in a soprano voice, and accompanied them to the Cadillac under his own power, walking with swaying hips.

At a stoplight, Brenda turned around to inspect Dow. "Why, he's *darling!*" she exclaimed.

"Hey," Dow said. "Who's the fat old chickie-babe?"

"Let's go," Sid said grimly. "We're running behind time."

Abruptly grim herself, Brenda drove on.

The Seniles converged on a towering smoky-glass cube on Sunset Boulevard in Hollywood. The hour was 6:25 P.M., and vehicular and pedestrian traffic were subsiding. Impersonating a prospective tenant for the new edifice, Biff had secured full details by telephone from a management which didn't yet have a full house, so everybody knew how to proceed; his information had been extensive enough to preclude the necessity of a dry run.

Sam and Biff stopped their truck in a yellow commercial zone, gathered tools, entered the lobby, and disappeared into an elevator. As they did, Brenda halted in the white passenger loading zone at the front of the building and discharged Bill, Dow and Sidney Ellen.

"Make a move or open your mouth, Ernestine," Sid said quietly, "and I'll blow your head off."

Again Dow rose to the occasion, steadied by Bill, and negotiated the sidewalk and lobby without incident. Directly behind them walked Sid, one hand in her open purse, grasping the automatic. A young man leaving the elevator which they awaited cast an appreciative eye on Dow, who was too stunned to notice.

As they rose in the elevator, he surfaced for a moment and said, "This is the only way to fly, man."

Management Associates Cartel occupied the fourteenth and fifteenth floors, at the top of the building.

Mort Zimbal's offices were at the rear of the west hall of floor fifteen, with his highest executives occupying rooms on either side toward the front and around in the east hall. On the fourteenth were accounting and other business departments.

The target area was fifteen, the west hall specifically. Biff and Sam were established midway in it beside the doors of the men's and women's toilets, tools scattered around, a portable oxyacetylene torch lighted and hissing, welder's hoods on their heads. Sam had started posting "out of order" signs on the toilet doors when Sid, Bill and Dow debouched from the elevator, went into the MAC reception rooms, passed the unoccupied receptionist's post, were ignored by the busy night telephone operator in a distant glassed enclosure, and hurried along the west hall. Haste caused Dow to stumble, and Bill grabbed him. Sid helped shove him into the women's toilet. Sam closed the door on them.

Waiting was nervewracking. Biff turned away two women and a man, recommending they try the still-operable rest rooms on the fourteenth floor. Sam, keeping up a pretense of going into and out of the men's room carrying tools, directed his attention to Zimbal's office. Several men and one woman entered at intervals, were evidently closeted with him, and departed. The time advanced to 7:05 P.M.

Sweat gathered under Biff's headgear, and he said, "Major, we can't wait forever."

"Ten more minutes," Sam told him. "It's thinning out. Don't spook."

In the women's room, Bill was inspecting himself in a mirror. "I'm too pale," he said. "I think I'll add rouge . . . I'm scared. How much longer is this going to last?"

Sid gave no answer, gripping her gun and setting her teeth. Bill dabbed at his cheeks. Their prisoner sat on a toilet in a stall, heavy-eyed and drooping.

Nobody came along the hall. The distant ringing of

telephones diminished. Sam's time limit was exceeded, and Biff shuffled his feet and made pleading noises that sounded hollow under his hood. Then a handsome, miniskirted young woman dashed from Zimbal's office, reached them, and voiced dismay.

"I'm sorry," Biff said. "We're having a real fight with the water pressure. Try downstairs. Are you from Mr. Zimbal's office?"

"Yes," she said.

"Could we go in and look at his private bathroom? I don't want it to go out on him."

"Yes. He's between appointments right now."

The young woman trotted toward the reception room and elevators.

"Okay," Sam said.

"Look out for the armed man he told me he'd have with him," Biff warned.

They ran to Zimbal's door. The large outer room, with desks for two secretaries, was empty, and the door to the inner room stood ajar. Zimbal looked up from his desk at the intruders without visible surprise. Sam's huge Army pistol seemed not to impress him.

"Thirty Industrials," Biff said. "Where's your guard?"

"Ah. Waiting in my car." Zimbal registered slight approval. "I didnt expect you here—or so soon."

"Come see Dow. Have you got the money?"

"Yes."

Biff led, Zimbal followed, and Sam, gun hidden, brought up the rear. The hall was deserted. Skirting the jetting torch, they crowded into the women's room. Sid retreated to a corner, automatic ready. Bill raised the debilitated prisoner from the toilet seat and brought him forward. Zimbal stared at him, face expressionless, and Dow gamely swished and smiled.

"Mort, baby," he said. "It's me. Don't bug me because I'm zonked out of my gourd, man. You know?"

"Jesus!" Zimbal said. He closed his eyes for a few seconds. "Very ingenious. . . . Come along."

Sam and Biff returned with him to his office. His secretary hadn't come back, and two telephones were buzzing and flashing. Zimbal picked them up in both hands, ignoring the emergence of Sam's gun. "Put everything on hold for ten minutes," he said.

He stepped to a wall bookcase, pulled aside a section precisely as they did in the movies, and turned the dial on a small safe door. Tumblers clicked, he moved a lever, and the door opened. Removing a big manila envelope, he gave it to Biff, who pried up the flap, peered at the currency through his faceguard, and began counting.

"Forget it," Sam said. "Mr. Zimbal knows better than to have a shortage."

"Correct," Zimbal said. "I pay my debts. Leave Jones in the toilet. I'll have my secretary get him. Will he need medical attention?"

"No," Sam said. He waved the gun. "But you're going back with him."

"I'm much too busy for dramatics. Run along."

Sam's eyes acquired the dark, hard shine of obsidian. "You lousy, faking bum. I hate your guts, and I'm looking for an excuse to kill you."

Zimbal blanched, his aplomb shaken. "Ah. Yes. I see. Certainly."

In the outer room they encountered Zimbal's secretary hastening to resume her duties. "Oh," she said, "Mr. Zimbal, I—"

"You go too, dear," Sam said.

"Oh, my God!"

Zimbal caught her arm and pulled her along. "Don't talk, Margie," he said. "This isn't as bad as it seems."

The hall was empty. Biff held open the door of the women's room for Zimbal and his secretary; he gave the envelope containing the money to Sam, who put it into a tool case and turned off the oxyacetylene torch. He joined the others.

Inside, Sid had the newcomers covered. Dow was

washing his face at a basin, supported by Bill. His makeup had run and one false eyelash had fallen off. Margie stopped and stared.

"My God!" she said.

"Got to tighten up," Dow said. "This has been a trip, Marge baby. Like Pan American around the world. You know?"

At an emphatic nod from Sam, Sid eased out, handed her pistol to him, and went rapidly along the hall, heels clicking, not venturing a backward look although Bill was supposed to be with her. As she waited for an elevator, she was consumed by worry and guilt about her failure to dispose of Golda.

Bill had hesitated when Sid left, and almost dropped the paper towel with which he was drying Dow's cheeks. He said softly: "Goodbye, Ernie."

"Hey, Uncle Rod," Dow said. "Don't go. We got to rap a little more."

"I'll never forget you," Bill said, and fled, surrendering the Walther en route to Sam.

Dow gazed after him in pained farewell. "He's not a chick," he explained. "Uncle Rod's in drag. Beautiful . . ."

As Bill was running to join Sid, the elevator arrived for her. Two well-groomed young men stepped out, and one politely held the doors for Sid. She thanked him. Bill glanced over his shoulder in alarm, but Sam and Biff had not come out of the women's room. He butted past the men, head down, and Sid pressed a button.

"The old ladies are getting tougher every day," one of the young men said to the other.

Back in the women's room Biff, protected by Sam's .45, seated Dow, Zimbal and Margie on toilets and tied their wrists and ankles with cords; then he prepared gags of gauze and tape.

"Confining us is sensible," Zimbal said, "but the rest of this is trying my patience."

"You've already tried mine," Biff said, and sank an

enormous hand into Zimbal's collar and tie and rocked him sharply; cloth and buttons ripped and popped. "I'm 'Dummy.' Remember?"

"Ah. My apologies."

"Quiet!" Sam said.

They heard voices in the hall, and a mention of "Mort." Men were talking. The sound faded out.

"Hey," Dow said. "You're the big dude that flattened me in Malibu—"

Biff cuffed him. Sam said, "No more conversation."

"Yeah?" Dow said. "Wait'll I start singing to the fuzz, man."

"Shut up, dummy!" Zimbal ordered.

The talking outside picked up, then dwindled; then silence fell. Biff applied gags. After surveying the hallway through the partially opened door, Sam motioned to Biff and they left the room. While Biff gathered up the tools, Sam hammered three tenpenny nails into the door and jamb. They removed their hoods and made for the elevators.

Around the block, Brenda picked up Sid and Bill. She was ten minutes late; having grown uneasy at the task of driving in the same area for so long, she had gone elsewhere and bought gasoline for the Cadillac. Sid got in beside her, and Bill settled in the rear.

"I was getting awfully worried," Brenda said.

"Go past the building," Sid said. "They ought to be coming out now. They've got the ransom."

All of them peered anxiously ahead through gathering darkness. Sam and Biff were finishing the loading of the pickup; they climbed a shade too quickly into the cab. No signs of recognition were exchanged as the big black car passed. The truck pulled out into the near lane, went only as far as the next intersection, and swung south.

"Success," Sid said. "So far." But she could not forget Golda and Harvey, alive and well and in the Malibu Colony, possibly already cuing the cops.

"I feel like crying," Bill said.

"So do I," Sid said. She wanted to add. "You would too—twice as hard—if you knew what I do."

"Well!" Brenda said. "This is a fine way to act when you're successful."

During the trip to Santa Monica, Bill sank to the rear floor, hid under a laprobe, and squirmed energetically. He emerged as his normal self. His discarded female clothing was wadded into a laundry bag. While he was busy, Sid abandoned her blond fall and white sweater, put on a coat and different slippers, peeled off false eyelashes and eyebrows, and resumed her normal makeup.

"Just in case," she said nervously, "drive around the block once before we stop for the Chevy."

They could make out nothing in the dark in the first sweep, and Brenda stopped next time. Bill transferred to the other car and drove off hurriedly.

"Bill seems terribly depressed," Brenda said. "What's wrong?"

"He's had a miscarriage," Sid replied. "He just lost his baby."

"You mean Jones?"

"Yes."

Brenda digested that. "Why, how awful! It's unnatural."

"Well, so is kidnapping."

The Cadillac followed the Chevrolet to Los Angeles International and circled the inner part of the airport; Bill signaled from the sidewalk in front of American Airlines, to which he had strolled after turning in the car, and was taken aboard. He said the transaction had been routine, that no one had noticed his change in appearance since renting the Chevrolet, and relapsed into glum silence.

Both Brenda and Sid were tired. The three rode in

silence to Long Beach, where they picked up Carter at the airport. He complained of his long wait.

"My goodness," Brenda said snippily. "How sad!"

"We're so *sorry* for you, Doctor," Bill said.

"Drop dead," Sid said.

"Bless me," Carter said, taken aback. "What a charming group you are. Have we made any money?"

"Who cares?" Bill said.

On the way to Redondo Beach, Brenda remarked, "I like driving, but this is ridiculous."

Sam and Biff were supposed to be awaiting them on a hilly street overlooking the sea, but there was a delay because of a misunderstanding about which block; presently the vehicles came together, after having to stall for passing traffic, and they shifted equipment to the Cadillac trunk. Biff and Sam were out of the coveralls and in suits, and Biff had removed his disguise. He took the wheel of the Tilden car and drove off with Sam and Sid. Their only communication was a few words from Sam, who said that he thought it had gone all right and that he was carrying the ransom. Brenda and Carter took over the pickup. The entire operation, after rendezvous, required three minutes.

"Carty," Brenda said, "do you think Sid killed the nosy maid next door? She didn't say, and I was afraid to ask her."

"Yes."

"Oh, dear!"

"My only regret," Carter said, "is that she couldn't have killed that lousy little songbird."

The night man at the truck rental agency in Inglewood, which also dealt in power tools, cement mixers, trailers and campers, was most obliging. He deducted five dollars from the fee on account of the return of the pickup on the same day. He offered to phone for a cab, but Brenda told him they couldn't afford one. She described the labors of their moving and how weary they were, and their appearance confirmed her story.

"The way inflation is cutting into most of us," the night man said, "before long we won't have enough to eat. I counted on Nixon to do something about prices, but all they've done is go up. Are you folks on a fixed income?"

"Well, not exactly," Carter said. "It varies from month to month."

"You're lucky."

"We have been so far."

Carter and Brenda walked limply for a couple of blocks, until Biff retrieved them. At Carter's instruction, Biff chauffeured them to a large, noisy restaurant on Pacific Coast Highway near Culver City. A pleasant girl in the foyer greeted them and provided a booth, into which they slid.

They felt no sense of jubilation, nor much fear; just fatigue, emptiness and some irritability. Listening to radio news broadcasts in the car had brought no enlightenment—either Dow, Mr. Zimbal and his secretary hadn't yet been discovered or the authorities were concealing information for their own purposes. By tacit agreement, nobody mentioned the nosy maid and her sinister absence from the news. At this moment their exploits seemed to them incredible and imagined; the money they had acquired seemed a fantasy.

Only Biff ordered a martini before dinner. The others weren't in a mood for celebration; the letdown after the events of the day was tremendous. Forcing a gaiety he did not feel, Carter held up his water tumbler.

"See here," he said. "This is an occasion for celebration, I think. Will you join me in drinking to a presumable success and confusion to the cops?

"I didn't kill her," Sid blurted. "I only tied her up."

They all stared, and Sid had to bite her lips to avoid

crying. Carter set down hard his untasted drink. Water slopped from it.

"Oh, God!" Bill said bitterly. "The *killer*."

"I'm glad," Brenda said, and patted Sid's arm. "I don't care a bit, dear."

"There goes my appetite," Biff said. "But it was gone anyhow."

"There will," Carter stated, "be no further discussion."

Brenda and Sid had creamed chicken on toast, Biff scrambled eggs, Bill a tomato stuffed with chicken, Sam an order of poached eggs, and Carter a bowl of clam chowder. Carter studied his companions gloomily. It occurred to him, as he questioned his wisdom and mourned his years and vanished teeth, that no mob had ever gathered together like this after pulling off a big job. Humphrey Bogart would have died laughing.

He longed to get Sidney Ellen and Bill to the airport and off to San Francisco and to go home to bed.

Underlings in MAC grew concerned at the mysterious absence of Mort Zimbal. Mrs. Zimbal telephoned his office and couldn't raise anyone. He had an appointment for dinner. Calls from London, Paris, Rome and New York remained unanswered.

At last someone heard shouting in the women's room on the fifteenth floor. A private detective hired by Zimbal to accompany him during ransom negotiations showed up, discovered the nails in the door, and had a janitor free it. Margie had managed to chew through her gag and was responsible for the yelling. For a brief period, being an attractive and leggy girl, she was the heroine of the Dow Jones story.

Although numb and cramped from his bonds and in a poor frame of mind, Zimbal swung immediately into action. He forbade calling the police until certain arrangements were completed; these included getting Denny Goodman to supervise public relations and conducting a thorough rehabilitation of Dow. It was very important, he emphasized, that their boy not confront the news media while still on a trip. And he had to shed his female garments. Dow protested, because he thought a return to his public in drag would be beautiful and sensational. Mr. Zimbal merely glared and called him a dummy.

Secluded in Zimbal's bathroom, Dow was stripped, bathed, provided with regular clothing sent from his home, and reunited with the four Averages, who were instructed by Goodman to weep when they publicly welcomed the restoration of their leader. Dow's hairdresser, snatched from revels in a gay bar on Hollywood Boulevard, was conveyed to the office in Zimbal's Rolls-Royce and changed his client from blond to brunette. Then a grueling briefing session, which embraced principals and witnesses, took place. Everybody was rehearsed in his lines. Dow, a quick study, submitted to editing and improvement of his recollections of captivity and release by Zimbal and Goodman. He went through a complete rehearsal of the revelations he was going to make.

Finally the cops, press, television and radio were notified. The fifteenth floor became a madhouse. These were Dow's best hours. He and a constantly growing entourage were up all night. Sirens wailed, all-points police bulletins were issued, TV floods glared, strobe lights flashed, cameras clicked and whirred, microphones were everywhere, commentators took to the air, guards were posted, walls, doors and toilets were dusted for fingerprints, a curious nocturnal floating population of hippies and sensation seekers and fans gathered outside the building, and a spokesman for the Federal Bureau of Investigation (the only man in the assemblage wearing a hat) said he had no comment.

If he could have suppressed many of the details of Dow's kidnapping, Zimbal would have done so. But that was impossible. Still, Goodman did manage to play down a great deal of the female impersonation aspect, and he eliminated references to the fact that Dow had been on what was a rather happy trip as well as the longest of his career. His heroic attempt to free himself by using karate on his captors was altered to the extent that he was in the end subdued by a pistol, not flattened with a punch from a senior citizen.

But the senior citizen aspect was very much a factor. Independently of Dow's discovery and report, neighbors had found Golda in the Malibu Colony house, her presence revealed by the barking of Harvey. Task forces of cops sped to the beach and hunted for suspects and fingerprints and interviewed bystanders. The gate guards were embarrassed at Dow Jones's having passed under their very eyes. Witnesses differed wildly on descriptions and details. The one firm license number available, that of the rental Chevrolet taken down as a matter of course by the men at the Malibu Colony gate, was presently traced to an agency at Los Angeles International, but the trail ended there. Nobody quite remembered the old guy who had rented it, and the credentials he had furnished were found to be false. A counter girl was by no means sure the same man who had taken it out was the man who had returned it. And one or both had vanished.

Golda rose to a brief, crazy eminence under cruel floodlights with cameras eyeing her and people listening to her every word. Even Harvey received marked attention, and assiduously begged in the crowd.

"You don't get nothing out of me," Golda cried. "Nothing! I promised Grandma. That's why she didn't shoot me. I wanted to join the gang. I may yet. Listen, you want me to squeal and get knocked off some night?"

The cops pleaded with her. They promised protection.

"Not me," Golda said. "I didn't see nobody. I don't know nothing. I thought Dow Jones was a girl. If

Grandma and Uncle Rod and the nurse and Dr. Morton was to come up to me the next minute, I wouldn't recognize them. I wasn't wearing my glasses, see?"

When pressed, she grew hysterical. Spirited away, booked as a material witness, sent to County Medical for a psychiatric examination, she had her cause espoused by a prominent criminal attorney, serving without fee, who mentioned flagrant violations of the First, Second and Fifth Amendments to the Constitution and disregard of the Bill of Rights, and threatened to secure a writ of *habeas corpus*.

Eventually she was permitted to go free, officially certified as being of mildly unsound mind. She never did prove of assistance to the police. One day, long before Miss Gallo returned from Europe, Golda received a plain envelope containing a sizable amount of crisp new banknotes. It had been mailed in San Diego. She remained silent about that, too.

Altogether, what investigators had didn't add up to a lot. Nobody in their mug books resembled the Grandma Bandit, assuming they were in possession of anything like an accurate description of her; she seemed to have a different look to everybody who had seen her. Uncle Rodney was a nothing, the male nurse a large and anonymous thug who could not really be described, and Dr. Morton a misty old buffer not listed in medical registers and unknown to fellow practitioners.

The actual abductors (probably not the Smiths) had been concealed under crash helmets and clothing hard to identify. New Thunderbirds like the one used by the doctor were plentiful in Southern California. Evidently the truck rental employees in Inglewood never connected the elderly couple moving to the Valley with the kidnappers, or else they didn't care to get involved; in any event, they did not come forward to throw any light on the small truck (license number unknown) driven by the men in coveralls bearing the name of a fictitious building maintenance firm. Fingerprints garnered by the cops failed to supply leads.

Dow gave a good description of a murderous Aunt Ethel, but was less sure of Uncle Rod, the male nurse, and the doctor. A most confusing circumstance was Uncle Rod's transvestism, and a question arose as to whether he might in fact be a she posing as a he to further foul up pursuers. Saying he couldn't be positive, Dow explained that he had been ill quite a lot of the time during his incarceration and had been suffering from a concussion after his fight for freedom, and that Uncle Rod had cared for him like a mother. That seemed to indicate Uncle Rod might have come from the distaff side.

Despite obvious goodwill, Mort Zimbal and his secretary were hardly more helpful—the two men wore welder's masks during the whole of Dow's delivery, and the two women in the toilet were shadowy figures who soon disappeared. Zimbal said the voice of the big man indicated he was the gang member who had conducted negotiations with him on the telephone, but the man had always muffled his voice, and it was not one ever heard before by Zimbal, and so he doubted that he could recognize it again. He had, of course, not seen the face of either man. One of the women could have been the Grandma Bandit, as Dow Jones stated, but Zimbal had paid practically no attention to her. He was unable to give a good description of her or Uncle Rod in his finery. Margie's testimony matched her boss's.

The number of people in the gang, and the sex of each, was uncertain. General agreement had them old. Witnesses who had seen them entering, inside, or leaving the building gave differing impressions, and in one instance confused Dow with Uncle Rodney or Grandma. Some consideration was given to the theory that Grandma might be male and superbly disguised.

Several investigators suspected that the aura of advanced years was itself a disguise. Grandma was given high marks for organizational ability and ferocity. It was widely conceded the gang was nonprofessional and without records, or anyhow new to this field of crime. A possibility existed that at least two, and possibly many, other jobs could be attributed to them. Their planning and execution were held to be first rate. Grandma was unquestionably the mastermind, male or female, a twisted genius, another Ma Barker or Alvin Karpis. That she headed a group of anti-establishment youths affecting age, was herself black or a communist or a student or the victim of drugs, had been under consideration.

"This thing is wide open," a detective lieutenant said, "up to and including the possibility that a bunch of old folks, without previouses and with a new approach, have got together to bust this town apart. We are withholding judgment."

Somewhat later, a police department spokesman said: "A full-scale investigation is proceeding. We expect to report progress."

An FBI man said files were never closed in the bureau until subjects were taken into custody and duly prosecuted. He looked competent and ominous and wore a hat.

Interest in the case rapidly declined after it became apparent nothing else was likely to happen. Some of those close to the scene waited for another shoe to drop. It didn't.

The bookings of Dow Jones and the Four Averages were sensational, and they outgrossed their rivals everywhere. Dow himself was a national figure. He started his first movie, on location in Yugoslavia, within four months. Before he left California a horde of his followers descended on Malibu to commemorate his time in bondage and clashed with police. Injuries were sustained on both sides; an offshore wind bearing clouds of tear gas felled numerous bathers and surfers; one hundred eighteen persons were arrested.

Mr. Zimbal related his feelings in a network television interview, saying: "Half a million dollars is little enough to pay for Dow Jones. He has become the hottest property in the entertainment world. From now on he will be guarded like the gold at Fort Knox. We at Management Associates Cartel are happy he was returned to us unharmed, and we are not interested in the pursuit of vengeance. I like to think his millions of admirers feel the same way."

After pondering the matter, the Internal Revenue Service ruled against MAC deducting the ransom payment as a business loss; whereupon MAC appealed the ruling and prepared to file suit in a federal court.

No public mention was ever made of how the list of serial numbers on the thousand-dollar bills was lost in the confusion of obtaining Dow's freedom.

Biff entered the Golden Years golf tournament and finished runner-up. He thought Brenda looked pretty clapped-out after the Dow thing, and his passion for her had declined.

Sam went on a short fishing trip to Baja California. He took along a Krag carbine to shoot sharks with.

Sidney Ellen devoted herself again to animal welfare. She made a substantial, anonymous contribution to an animal shelter in Orange County.

Bill bought a Marie Laurencin, small but framed exquisitely, and hung it at the foot of the lower bunk in his trailer.

It was consolingly dull at first, and then just dull.

One night, having observed a prudent interval, the Tildens gathered their friends at a table at the country club to celebrate their forthcoming trip to Europe, which they told everybody they had long dreamed of and saved up for. The occasion was gay. The Seniles had margaritas or frozen daquiris and drank a few discreet toasts—to the fuzz and a decaying civilization and the pleasures of squaring accounts and even to the few benefits accruing to the aging process. And, naturally, to Dr. Tilden's well-stuffed back brace, which was going with him to Zurich and the Grundich et Cie Bank.

All around them were old crocks, chatting emptily and getting smashed and dancing feebly, resigned to programmed lives of community activities, tending gardens, collecting antiques and going to doctors. In such an atmosphere their secret identities and deeds were incomparably delicious. They could not help but speculate on how a disclosure of what they had done would rock Golden Years. Yet in their satisfaction was a measure of sadness; it was ostensibly over.

Carter sounded elegiacal when he said, "It was easy. Easier than I ever imagined. If only ten per cent of the population were honest, it would be far harder. Or if the cops knew what to do."

"I wish you were younger, Carty," Brenda said. "We could have had a yacht."

She was vivid and gay—having been promised a week in Italy and a chance to meet the Commendatore and order a new red Ferrari—and svelte in a short black dinner dress that bulged a little at the seams. Gazing at her, Biff thought she had never been lovelier and felt suddenly rejuvenated.

There was some talk of spending the profits. A first requirement for that was the leaving of Golden Years. Nobody had any plans, and Carter regarded them with knitted brows.

"Why?" he asked. "You should enjoy your riches— you worked for them. What's the sense to leaving the money to relatives, or possibly to the government, or forgotten in a Swiss bank?"

After a silence, Sid said, "Well, I sort of hate to leave Journey's End. . . ."

"Why?" he demanded. "Isn't that what you were trying to escape in the first place?"

"Yes."

"Then you've taken leave of your senses. Why do you want to stay on?"

"Because it's a good cover," Sid blurted.

"Absolutely, luv," Bill added, with an abrupt, hopeful cheeriness. "We know the territory."

Carter stared at Sam and perceived that the old fool was smiling. "Good heavens!" he said. "So that's what has been going on behind my back."

"No, it's spontaneous," Sam said. "We haven't discussed this among ourselves. Right?"

The others murmured assent.

"No," Carter said. "No, sir! I'd never live through another job." He turned to Biff. "You're not a party to this, are you?"

"Oh, I might be," Biff said. "You don't want to live forever, do you, Doctor?"

"Listen, Carter," Sam said. "Have your vacation. Enjoy yourself. Take your time. Recharge your batteries. We'll be waiting for you."

"I'll never come back," Carter said.

"Of course you will, Carty," Brenda told him. "As soon as your batteries are better. Then we'll have some more fun."

"Fun . . ." Carter said.

Then a menacing, unlawful, exciting, hopeful, intoxicating gerontological warmth bathed his bones, despite arthritic twinges and a warning of risen blood pressure in his ears. This was his mob. He was conscious of a pride of position and achievement.

"Well," he said, "if something interesting comes up someday, I suppose we can look into it."

Order by Mail —

MYSTERY & SUSPENSE

THAT'S NO WAY TO DIE, by Lamar Kelley. A man was brutally beaten to death, but it was termed "accidental." The same for a young boy forcibly drowned . . . and for a beautiful woman. Yet one man was determined to prove these deaths were murders.
X2148-60¢

MADAME MAIGRET'S OWN CASE, by Georges Simenon. It was Madame Maigret who stumbled onto the body in the bookbinder's furnace . . . and was lead with her husband along a devious path straight to the solution of an "impossible" crime. T2425-75¢

THE MEN WHO EXPLAINED MIRACLES, by John Dickson Carr. "The year's most distinguished mystery collection" (N. Y. TIMES) contains seven "impossible" crimes brilliantly presented and miraculously solved by favorite heroes. T2224-75¢

THE RED RIGHT HAND, by Joel Rogers. Everyone knew the ugly little red-eyed man with dog-pointed teeth and twisted legs had committed a murder . . . but only one man was willing to prove it, even though it meant his life might end! T2223-75¢

MURDER COMES HOME, by Anthony Gilbert. A corpse in a curious costume leads the indefatigable Arthur Crook on the most baffling case of his career. T2373-75¢

FLASHBACK, by Roger Dooley. An intriguing, well-plotted whodunit written entirely from the author's own experiences with Hollywood, aging movie stars, decrepit bars and murder. T2395-75¢

DOSSIER IX, by Barry Weil. An Israeli secret agent must find an escaped master spy, break up an espionage ring, and head off a nuclear holocaust . . . in one of the freakiest, fast-moving spy thrillers of the year. N2243-95¢

HOOLIGAN, by David Dodge. A new and brutal brand of secret agent chases 100-million dollars through the snakepits of Hong Kong and discovers a brutal, chilling truth in this unusual adult spy novel. T2320-75¢

YOU CAN'T LIVE FOREVER, by Harold Q. Masur. Scott Jordan, lawyer and private eye, finds sex and scandal backstage on Broadway. Then, murder steals the show. T2340-75¢

OPERATION S-L, by Norman Daniels. Naked passion and razor-edged espionage set in an African death trap with international double-bedding and triple-crossing that left little hope for John Keith of his ever getting out alive. T2415-75¢

TO ORDER PYRAMID BOOKS BY MAIL:
1. Circle the number of each book you are ordering.
2. Complete all information.
3. Detach coupon and send with your remittance to:
PYRAMID BOOKS, M.O. Dept.
9 Garden Street, Moonachie, N.J. 07074

6R

NAME

ADDRESS

CITY _____ STATE _____ ZIP _____

X2148-60¢ T2425-75¢ T2224-75¢ T2223-75¢ T2373-75¢
T2395-75¢ N2243-95¢ T2320-75¢ T2340-75¢ T2415-75¢

I ENCLOSE $ _____ (NOTE: Pyramid pays postage and handling on all orders for $5.00 or more. On orders for less than $5.00, please add 10c per book.) Please allow three to four weeks for delivery.